SHADOW RANGE

SHADOW RANGE

Curtis Bishop

GUNSMOKE

This hardback edition 2010
by BBC Audiobooks Ltd
by arrangement with
Golden West Literary Agency

ISBN 978 1 408 46252 2

British Library Cataloguing in Publication Data available.

Printed and bound in Great Britain by
CPI Antony Rowe, Chippenham and Eastbourne

To MIKE—*and luck on the trail.*

1

BEN ANTHONY was surprised to find a half-dozen horses tethered in front of the Wide S gate, and to recognize as many neighboring brands, even Fritz Warner's Square Diamond. Evidently there was some kind of meeting at Walter Earnest's, for so many ranchmen would not be dropping over just for a visit.

And certainly not Fritz Warner.

Ben turned back to his horse and had started to remount when Elizabeth Earnest called out from the well in the front yard. He had not seen her there among the cottonwoods planted twenty years before by a woman who could not bear to live in a house without surrounding shade trees.

And Elizabeth came out to the gate to meet him, a tall slim girl with wide serious blue eyes and a firm mouth, an aloof sort of girl with none of a woman's artificialities in speech or manner, but enough of a woman with her ruddy complexion and her slender curved body to stir a man's blood, and to make him wish there was a different kind of look in her calm eyes—for him, at least.

But Ben Anthony's broad face showed nothing of the reaction he felt. In this sense Ben was a colorless sort of man. Giving him a cordial greeting, smiling a welcome, and shaking his hand, Elizabeth noticed again how big he was, how much like an easygoing thick-headed hulk he looked, with even the lazy slow smile of a man who is big and good-natured but has little besides his animal strength and his affability to recommend him. And she thought how deceptive that was, how surprised even those who had known Ben Anthony the longest, herself and Walter Earnest, still were by his ambition and his shrewd capacity for trading.

"What was your rush, stranger?" she demanded. "Seems like,

I

every time I see you lately, you're taking off like a sage hen."

"I've been making tracks," he admitted. "However, there's no rush. I just noticed the horses, and didn't want to break up anything inside. It looks like a powwow. No place for an honest freighter."

Bess nodded. "They've been palavering for over an hour." She waited a moment. "I'm worried, Ben. Sick with worry. Dad let his last hand go today. And Marvin Sledge tells us he's as flat as one of your pancakes."

"That's some flat," Ben admitted, " 'cause I cook the best pancakes in this country." His tone was light, but his look and his expression were serious. "I didn't know Walt was that bad off," he added in a different tone. "I offered the old buzzard all the money he needed to get through this winter."

"Walt Earnest take a loan from you!" Bess exclaimed. Her tone was half reproof of Ben for having such an idea, half scorn of her father for refusing. "You know him, Ben. We'll get by till spring, on our credit at Morgan Mann's. Then, if cattle are still dirt-cheap, we're wiped out."

"And Walt, I suppose, won't talk of selling hides and tallow?"

"No."

Bess added after a moment of thought, "Selling hides and tallow won't keep a ranch going."

"Guess not," Ben admitted. He did not add what he was thinking, that sometimes a man had an ache in his abdomen instead of a stomach, and that then a man would sell anything to still that pain.

"Go on in," Bess said, nodding toward the house. "One more in the pot won't hurt. Besides, Walt will want to see you."

Ben swung his big frame over the two-strand wire fence, not bothering with the board gate. He could hear the voices even this far off, and Walt Earnest was talking loudest. There had been rumors for days of such a meeting. A year ago all of the ranchmen grazing stock in the Chin-chin basin could not have met in one house, but their numbers had dwindled in these twelve months. And more were about to go.

This was the second of the cattle country's darkest years. Other ranges had been hit hard in '73, when no man had been able to make ends meet going up the trail. The nearness to Gulf ports, and the economy of shipping, had helped out this country. But in '74 even that had been impractical. Now, in the autumn of '75, there was no demand for beef at all.

It didn't make sense. The world was the same, and people had to have food to live. What were they eating? For a decade or more Texas beef had filled their stomachs. Now, of a sudden, Texas beef wasn't worth the cost of getting it to market. Of a sudden a stripped cowhide and what little tallow a lean range steer produced was worth more than the live animal.

Walt Earnest even, Walt Earnest of the Single Bob and the Wide S, was flat. His own daughter said so. Worrying about a mere detail of life like groceries. Walt Earnest, who had ordered his boots hand-sewn in San Antonio and his saddle studded with brass and silver. Walt Earnest, who had dominated this Alice country with a loving, yet bullying hand; who had given a home to a young waif named Ben Anthony; who had even offered, five years before, to set Ben up with a spread of his own.

Ben stopped on the porch to roll a smoke before going inside, and brooded over the irony of it. Walt Earnest down to living on his credit at Morgan Mann's! It was on this same porch, five years before, that he had talked like a father to Ben Anthony, with all of the short impatience of a father. Ben was throwing over a good riding job to speculate on cattle, to buy and sell. "No man ever got anywhere trading, except a damned Yankee," Walt Earnest had declaimed. "Land, Ben, is the only thing worth living for. It's the only medium of exchange that means the same year after year. A man starts trading. He profits, and he loses. All he ever has is temporary possession of a worthless dollar. But land grows on a man, and a man grows with the land. In good years he can buy more. In bad years he has what is his own under his feet."

Since that day Ben Anthony had made money driving herds north, had come back to Texas to set up his freight and stage line that was the only means of public transportation over an area drained by three big rivers, and embracing the civilizations of two countries. And now, of course, he could hand some of the old man's advice back to him. He could, if he felt like it, call Walt Earnest out onto this same porch and ask, "Who's a sucker?" and

3

gloat with the triumph of a man who made his own bed, and that a soft one.

But nothing was further from Ben's mind as he hesitated with his hand on the door. There had been things he could not tell Walt Earnest because Walt was Elizabeth's father. For a long time Ben had yearned for the comfort and dignity of a ranch like the Wide S, for the security, even so insecure, of land under his feet. He did still. But, in such a short time, this country had lost its wildness, and its open range character. In such a short time men had swallowed up all the open country there was, and even had begun to fight among themselves because there wasn't enough. In such a short time there had come to be two classes of men and young men: those who hadn't, and those who had. The land had all been taken up, until a button like Ben Anthony could not find a foothold. He could have ridden on, to Arizona or Wyoming. Tales drifted back from those regions of land that was still free and new. But something brought him back to this Chin-chin basin, and held him here, where he could never own what he wanted. A part of that something, more than he had ever admitted to himself, more than he could have admitted to Walt Earnest even if his life had depended upon it, was Bess Earnest.

Ben thrust open the door and gave the men present the slow grin that made him look more than ever like a big good-natured mammal who could never be quick nor capable in anything except acts of physical violence.

"Come in this house, Ben," roared Walt Earnest, leaping out of his cane-backed chair. There was no way of knowing how many men, some of them complete strangers, Walt Earnest had roared that to. And meant it.

The Wide S owner was tall and stooped from long hours in the saddle. His white mustaches dropped away from his ruddy face like dry palm leaves from a sun-scorched trunk, but his eyes were as beady and keen as they had been forty years ago, when he had first talked with Texas men and drunk with them, in the market square at Washington-on-the-Brazos while huzzas rang out for Davy Crockett and his boys from Tennessee. Three wars had Walt Earnest fought in and through—three wars, that is, that historians would recognize. There had been other wars; this Wide S ranch had been built up by a man who could meet any challenge that came. Every man here, in fact, except glum Fritz Warner, knew of gun-fighting. The law that had come to this country was still new, and at times its cost came too high—in money. There was seldom enough of that. There was only a plenty of land and of human lives.

"Don't want to break up the meeting, Walt," Ben said hurriedly. Walt Earnest was old enough to be his father and, indeed, was the nearest thing to a father he had ever known, but it wasn't the way of this informal man-to-man world to call a man anything but his first or his last name.

"Meeting's just about over," Walt shrugged.

Harry Odell came out of an inside door and grinned.

"Come on in here," he ordered Ben. "I don't want you wandering around the yard with my gal."

Ben's face brightened, and he was quick with his joking reply. All of these men in Walt Earnest's living room were his friends, in an everyday sort of way. He had their approval because he showed good business judgment, and because he was honest and friendly in his dealings. But Harry Odell was the type of friend a man has but once. He and Ben Anthony had played and worked together as boys. And Ben, quick with his loyalty and unshakable when his devotion was once given, was utterly deaf to what other men in the valley were beginning to whisper—that Odell's Dollar Mark ranch was doing surprisingly well in a time when no honest ranchman could hold his head above water.

Ben said "Howdy," and that included them all: the Camerons, John and Martin and Alan; the Maitlands, Keith and Rex; tight-lipped, surly Fritz Warner, the man who they said squeezed a dollar until it oozed blood; bespectacled owlish Marvin Sledge, the banker; and big genial Morgan Mann, whose general store in Alice served outfits more than a day's ride away.

"We should be like Ben here," mused Morgan, "and not have any money worries. He was smart."

Ben Anthony shrugged off the compliment, at least outwardly. But he couldn't help a momentary glow of pride at the way these other men concurred in that respect. Nobody had ever thought the waif who settled at the Wide S ranch would ever amount to more than a good rider. They had given him credit for the qualities he had shown as a boy: a way with wild horses, a de-

5

pendability on his job, a quick and good judgment with a calf. They had even tried to hire him away from Walt Earnest. But when he had quit the Wide S all of them had shared Walt's opinion, that he was riding to ruin. None had conceded him what they now granted by acclamation: a business sense, an ambition, shrewd calculation.

That particularly shown in Marvin Sledge's eyes. Perhaps Sledge actually respected Anthony more than the others. Sledge was a man who would naturally admire dollar sense over all other qualities.

"You'd better see about borrowing dough from Anthony here," Sledge said in his cracked voice. "He's got more money than the bank."

"I think we can make out," Walt said from the doorway. He hesitated, and seemed to look to Keith Maitland for approval.

Maitland looked quickly away as if knowing what he was asking, and not wishing to take the responsibility. Walt evidently decided to take Ben Anthony into his confidence, and theirs, without further speculation. Anthony was their friend, no doubt of that. But he did not belong to that class which had quickly sprung up in this cattle country: he owned neither land nor a brand.

"We're forming an association, Ben," Walt explained. "All of us have had to let our riders go. Most of us couldn't even pay up back wages. Harry there is able to keep three boys, God knows how. But the rest of us have got to do our own riding like we did when we were buttons. We're making this a free range until this panic is over. That's the only way we can fight Caddo Parker and his wolves."

Ben nodded. He knew their troubles. There were no rustlers in this valley, not as they had once thought of rustling. No steer was worth the trouble of stealing with prices this low. But gangs were sweeping through the ranches killing stock wantonly, stripping their hides then and there, until at Corpus Christi and at Port Isabel there were dry hides stacked up higher than a man's head waiting for shipment.

Ben held back the question he wanted to ask. This, on the surface, was a free and easy land, where strangers were greeted with a cordial Howdy. But, underneath, was the age-old suspicion of one man for his fellow man, plus an independence developed by time and by space. He wanted to ask what about Marvin Sledge, who had fashioned tallow vats on his own ranch, who was shipping hides and tallow to Port Isabel in Ben's wagons.

The banker seemed to sense this thought, though Ben did not as much as glance in his direction. "You can help us, Ben," said the scrawny little man. "Some hides and tallow will continue to go out of this valley. I have had to foreclose on some herds, and I guess others will come to me. But you can refuse to accept hides for shipment unless there is a bill of sale from the owner of the brand."

"That," squirmed Ben, "is making me responsible. I'll do what I can. I'll take none of Caddo Parker's hides unless there is a bill of sale."

"I wish Ben were riding for us," said Keith Maitland. "Parker was down in my lower pasture last night. The —— —— doesn't even bother to conceal his tracks."

Harry Odell stood up again. If he was uncomfortable under the hinted suspicion of some of these men, he did not show it.

"I'm with you as far as a free range is concerned," he said. "I have three riders. We'll take the ridge leading up to the pass. That's the hardest riding. But my lower range is overstocked, and it's only fair to tell you I'm selling off some culls. At the best price I can get."

His dark eyes flickered a challenge to Keith and Rex Maitland. Lean ruddy men, the Maitlands. Perhaps the most dangerous men in the valley, for their tempers could blaze the highest. And nothing, not even a salty Brahma calf, was as stubborn as a Maitland.

"That's your business," Keith Maitland answered curtly.

"Men, whatever else, we've got to carry stockers until spring," Walt Earnest appealed. "Even if we half starve. This will be over by spring. I talked to Gilbert Henry in San Antone, and he tells me meat isn't getting to the crossroads stores, and that the Army will buy up plenty of beef in the spring. Mebbe you know about that, Ben. Have you gotten a hint of any Army buying?"

"No," Ben said regretfully. "Army freighting has dropped off. I carried two loads from Brownsville to San Antone last week. That's all this month."

7

"I can carry you men for your groceries," confirmed Morgan Mann, the storekeeper. Unlike Sledge, Mann did not have a finger in every pie. He was a store man, and that was all. "Don't ask me how, but I'll do it some way. Ben there has a wagonload of stuff in his shed which I ain't paid out yet. I can't."

"I'll deliver it to you in the morning," Anthony offered quickly. "I didn't know that was what you were waiting on. When I got to turn you down for credit, Morgan, I'll go out of business."

"You're a freighter, not a moneylender," Morgan answered. "But I'll pay you interest, lad, if you can carry it."

"Interest be damned!" exploded Ben.

"That's the spirit, lad," Walt Earnest approved. "With that kind of feeling among us, we'll lick this winter. We'll lick Caddo Parker. I'll be up at daybreak riding my south pastures, and going as far as the spring on your land, Keith. I'm shooting at any and all riders I can't recognize. And I think I can still draw a bead."

There were answering echoes.

"Every man's troubles are his neighbor's," Walt went on. "Sleep with one eye open, we gotta. When we hear shooting, pull on our boots and ride like hell. No use of looking to the Sheriff for help. Nobody has paid our taxes, and he can't keep a deputy working. It's up to us. And that's as it should be. We fought for this country once, and we can do it again."

"I'll see about getting money in San Antone," promised Sledge. "You men know, if I can get my hands on it, I'll let you have it. But already I'm in over my head. I've traded some of your notes off at a discount. I'll never foreclose, you know that. But the loan company will. I'd say next spring is your dead line. If you can't buy back your paper by then—"

The banker shrugged his shoulders in lieu of further prediction.

"We'll buy it back," Alan Cameron promised.

He had Walter Earnest's grim determination. His two sons nodded. Ben Anthony mused that the Camerons would be good men to have around in a fight.

They had grown up together in this sprawling creek-fed valley, three families, three cattle dynasties. Yet Ben wondered if this was not the first time the Maitlands, the Camerons and the Earnests had met in one house, and on completely friendly terms. Fritz

8

Warner did not matter, nor Harry Odell, though Harry's Dollar Mark was a brand as old and his range was richer in rainy years.

It was hard to believe that once a Maitland had killed a Cameron, and that Walt Earnest had winged Keith himself with a rifle, and that Ben Anthony as a button had carried a six-gun with orders from Walt to shoot on sight any Cameron rider seen on the Wide S side of the gnarled, twisting mile-wide ridge which, in this valley, had been a no man's land.

Now the meeting broke up. Fritz Warner came over to Ben.

"Did you get in some fence material for me today, Mr. Anthony?" he asked.

He was always like that, mistering his neighbors, speaking only when speech was absolutely necessary. But there was something deep in Fritz Warner's eyes which showed that he was no groveling weakling. He had taken a nester's patch, and he had clung to it where other homesteaders had been chased away, or burned out, or at times manhandled if they showed defiance. It was a miracle of a decade ago that Fritz Warner had been permitted to stay at all; now, after ten years, not all of them good ones, it was another miracle that he was still here of his own volition, and that his one-man spread with only an upper finger of the valley to graze his stock upon was still operating.

Slowly respect for Warner's industry and frugality was increasing. Men such as the Maitlands and Walt Earnest would never like him, for he was not a ranchman. He was not quick and generous with his friendship or with his temper. He was not convivial and interesting in his talk. He owned cattle because cattle made him a living, not because possession of his own brand and his own herd made him feel like a king.

"Yes, Fritz," Ben nodded. Perhaps he came nearer than anybody else to actual friendship with the nester. And yet he too held something back.

"I'll ride in for it in the morning," Fritz promised. "The buckboard will carry everything, won't it?"

"Yes," Ben confirmed.

Now Marvin Sledge was plucking at his shoulder. "Riding back to town, Ben? I'll keep you company."

Ben considered this. Sledge was not a man to seek out another man's company because of loneliness. Nor could he conceal his eagerness when he wanted something.

"Stay for supper, Ben," Earnest said cordially. "All of you boys stay. We got a saddle of venison, and Bessie will throw out biscuits faster than you can dip 'em in gravy."

The Maitlands and the Camerons refused and started for their horses. They had agreed readily to a free range, and they would trust Walt Earnest until spring as he would trust them. But not yet were they willing to eat the Wide S fare, or have Walt Earnest "dig into" theirs.

"No," Ben declined, "I'll get on back. Stage busted a spring, and I gotta see if it's ready to roll."

"The fool works all the time," grinned Harry Odell. "He's got a half-dozen hands hanging around, but he still fixes springs himself and shoes his own horses. You'll never be anything but a working man, Ben."

"I'd rather have Ben Anthony shoe my mounts than any man in this country," Walt Earnest said shortly.

It was all too plain that Walt preferred Ben to this slim dark man who was his neighbor, and who would marry his daughter. Odell stared back at Walt a moment and then, with a shrug of his shoulders, went outside.

"Business holding up, son?" Walt asked.

"Dropping a little," Ben said. "No Army contracts until spring. But I get drivers cheaper. Everybody wants to work for me."

"It broke me up to let my hands go," Walt sighed. "I guess every rider in this country is looking for a job."

"And milling around saloons," Ben added. "Caddo Parker can be plumb choosy about the hands he takes on. . . . I'm ready, Marvin."

Harry Odell and Bess Earnest were talking by the well. She was sitting on the stone rim, her chin on her elbows, her eyes looking off over the slope of land that dropped in slow gentle rolls from the hill where the house stood to the narrow muddy streak that was Chin-chin Creek. She stood up as she saw Ben leaving, and she came almost to Harry's chin.

She called out in protest against Ben's leaving, interrupting Harry's talk.

"I thought you'd stay for supper," she said.

"No," he grinned, walking toward her. "Old Harry goes green with jealousy every time I ride up."

Once Ben had been unable to make small talk like that. Riding away from the Wide S, up the trail to the boom cities and back again, had taught him some things. But he was still a little self-conscious before Bess. Especially if Harry was around.

"I guess," she smiled, "Harry is the most jealous man I know."

"Of Ben, yeah," drawled Odell, not leaving his seat on the well rim. "He makes too much money to be trusted."

"You'll come again?" she asked. "We don't see enough of you lately, Ben. Every time I come to town and ask about you, you're off at San Antonio or Brownsville."

"I've been jumping," Ben admitted. "Gotta rustle business these days. Wait till spring and the Army dumps lush contracts in my lap, and I'll rest up." He turned to his horse with a light "So long."

Sledge was already in the saddle, sitting nervously, shoulders hunched forward. The banker would never be at home on a horse and would never pretend so. Ben's bay tossed up its sleek head and pretended to take a swipe at its owner. Sledge's mare squealed and leaped ten feet away. The banker groaned.

"Watch that killer, Ben."

Ben Anthony chuckled. Men like Sledge could never understand horses. And had no business riding them. The bay bucked a moment before settling into an even lope.

"I wouldn't have a horse like that around my place," growled Sledge.

"He just gets fidgety," Ben explained, patting the bay's rump. "Just hates to waste time hanging around gates. Why, this horse is as gentle as a baby."

"Don't tell me that!" protested Sledge.

They rode a mile in silence except for Ben's low chuckle. Then the banker slowed his horse down to a trot.

"You're missing the chance of a lifetime, Ben," he pointed out.

"Yeah? How?"

"Some of these spreads are going under. Most of 'em. I think Harry Odell will keep on a cash basis. But the Camerons and the Maitlands and even old Walt Earnest won't last another year."

"Does look rough," Ben admitted. "But what's that got to do with me? I'm running a freight line and some stagecoaches."

"They're in debt deep and going deeper," said Sledge. "I own enough of their paper to ruin 'em. I own too much of it, Ben. I'm in deeper than I'd like to be. I can't use all of this land. Some of it, yes. But not Maitland's spread. I couldn't get across the ridge and the canyon to work it."

"No," Ben conceded. Sometimes there were natural barriers to a man's ambition and greed.

"Now you"—Sledge's voice took on a shrill note as he tried argument—"you're young. You need a spread of your own. You've got money. You can buy paper from me, Ben. I'll sell some of Maitland's notes. Then, in the spring, you can move in when he busts up."

"I couldn't do that."

For a moment, though, Ben's heart leaped at the idea. Yes, he had money. Perhaps he could buy into the royalty of this valley, for a man who owned grass and a brand was that—even Fritz Warner was that—while a man who only had money was just another passing man.

"Why not?" Sledge snapped. "Who's to stop you?"

"Oh, I just couldn't," Ben said evasively. And lightly. So lightly that Sledge should have been warned against pursuing this subject further.

But the banker wasn't warned. Sledge was a little peeved that Ben, for a second time, wouldn't come around to his point of view. No other man in this cattle country would, except an isolated case here and there that Sledge did not want to talk about. Ranchmen thought of the dollar not as a glittering reality but merely as a symbol, and were scornful of Sledge's advice and ideas. Grass to them was all-important, dollars nothing—except when they needed money. Even then they asked for loans in a condescending manner, as if it was the predestined fate of a man such as Sledge to grant favors, but to ask none in return. Ranchmen couldn't see that dollars meant grass, and that grass meant dollars. The two were interchangeable. One was worthless without the other.

"I could fix it up to where most of the people wouldn't know you and me worked it," Sledge said eagerly. "I've had to juggle my papers some. I'm just a small man; I can't carry it all. The Cattlemen's Loan Association won't fool around with these men after spring shipping. You could turn the money over to me, Anthony. Deposit it in my bank. I'll lend it out for you to the Maitlands or the Camerons, mebbe both. Then I can shift that paper to the Loan Association. When they foreclose, you'll get first chance to buy up. And you'll already have the range paid for."

Ben Anthony's lips tightened.

"What's wrong with that set-up?" the banker demanded. "I tell you, Ben, it's the chance of a lifetime."

"It won't work, Sledge," Ben said coldly.

"Why not?"

"In the first place, I don't want a spread that way."

"Nothing dishonest about it," Sledge growled. "It's just business, Anthony."

Ben forced himself to hold back his anger. Marvin Sledge was trying to do him a favor, he was sure of that. He was sure also that, in Sledge's books, this wasn't underhanded dealing. Men had different codes, and he liked to concede every other man the right to a different opinion from his.

"We won't argue that," he said curtly. "You go ahead. Maybe it's all right for you. You don't think like I do."

"I'm a businessman," shrugged Sledge, "and when I see a chance—"

"The chance is here," Ben agreed. "But you're forgetting something, Sledge."

"What?"

"Say I bought the paper. Say the bank foreclosed. Who would get the Maitlands off for me?"

"What!"

"Just that. Who would move 'em off?"

"Why, the Sheriff," retorted Sledge. "The Sheriff would go out and give 'em notice to vacate. Say thirty days. Then you could move right in and all the improvements—"

"That's where you'll fail in this country, Sledge," Ben Anthony broke in. It was presumption for so young a man, who had spent his boyhood as a ranch hand, to give such advice to a businessman who was rich and was getting richer. "You don't know this country," he went on. "I hold no love for the Maitlands. But I'd ride out to fight for 'em against a Sheriff who tried to put 'em off. There'd be Walt Earnest there, and all of the Camerons. If times had picked up, they'd have their riders with 'em. I don't think any Sheriff of Jim Wells County would face that pack."

"It's the law," Marvin Sledge insisted. "Those men won't disobey the law."

"They'll be there on those spreads when you are gone and Caddo Parker is gone," Ben snapped. "There'll be a Maitland and a Cameron and an Odell working cattle in the Chin-chin valley when I'm gone. Try to buck that game, Sledge, and you'll lose every chip you got."

"You're a fool, Ben Anthony," Sledge said angrily. "I tell you there is law and order in this country. I tell you—"

Ben pulled up his horse. "I'll wait around for Morgan Mann," he said. "Got something to palaver with him about."

Sledge looked at the big man with narrowing eyes. He was warned by what he saw in Anthony's face.

"I was just trying to give you a push, Ben," he whined.

"Sure," Ben nodded. "I'm much obliged, Marvin. I'll be seeing you." And he turned his bay back up the trail to await Morgan Mann.

There was no reason why he should be angry. Marvin Sledge had merely approached him with a business proposition that was legitimate. As legitimate, Ben Anthony was willing to concede, as the deal he had pulled on a rival freight line operating out of Brownsville. But, to Ben if not to Sledge, there was a difference.

There was to other men. Ben chuckled aloud.

"I wouldn't want the Sheriff's job when Sledge starts foreclosing," he said to himself. A range was not bought with money, but with blood and sweat.

He heard Morgan coming and pulled up to wait. The storekeeper came over the rise, almost as big as the paint he was riding. He sat a horse no more gracefully than Marvin Sledge. He did not belong in a saddle, but behind a store counter, with a white apron gathered around his broad girth.

"Glad you waited, Ben," puffed Morgan. "Need somebody along if this fool cayuse decides to act up."

14

"After carrying your carcass this far," grinned Ben, "he ain't got the spirit."

Morgan never rode faster than at a gentle trot, and Ben held down the bay's gait to just keep up.

Neither spoke for a moment. Finally Ben blurted out:

"How is old Walt's account?"

"Shouldn't talk about my customers, Ben," Morgan gently reproved him. But then, after a brief hesitation, the storekeeper added: "But I reckon I can guess at your motive. Walt ain't paid me in two years, Ben. And he still feeds people high, wide, and handsome. I ain't added up his bill lately. It would run me crazy if I knew what the total is."

Ben nodded. That was Walt Earnest. The Earnest table was always groaning under the weight of food . . . Canned foods and fruits that nobody else in the valley ever thought about. And it was a rare day that the Wide S did not have company for dinner and supper.

"I'll bring you over a thousand in the morning," he said. "That'll carry Walt through the winter, won't it?"

"I ain't got no right to take your money against Walt's account," Morgan objected. Then, with a chuckle: "But it's either that or owe you myself. Bring it over, Ben."

Ben nodded. Morgan shot a sidewise look at his younger companion.

"You're all wool and a yard wide, son," he murmured.

"Hell!" Ben snapped. "He raised me from a button. I don't reckon I could do enough for Walt Earnest."

"Still," insisted Morgan, "old Walt ain't too easy to live with. I remember him chomping at the bit when you rode off on that cattle deal. Said if he was ten years younger he'd tan your hide."

"He would have tried it," Ben grinned, "only I didn't let him get ahold of me."

2

BEN ANTHONY stepped across the dusty street, pulling his drooping hat over his eyes against the head of the afternoon sun. As if admitting to the world that he was not a ranchman, he wore neither the expensive hat nor the hand-sewn boots which distinguished a breed, and a class of breed. There was nothing impressive about his appearance except his size, and that was deceptive—it was hard to see in him the surging power and shrewdness which had enabled him to start from nothing, and accomplish so much. His wagons and his stages covered a winding dusty road over three hundred miles long, and shot off into bypaths, to Corpus Christi and to Port Isabel, even to Galveston and Nuevo Laredo.

Only Ben Anthony knew why Alice was his headquarters town instead of San Antonio or Brownsville, or Port Isabel where the tugs plying the Gulf Coast chugged into harbor. Once, when asked bluntly, he murmured that his overhead was cheaper here, and that there were fewer temptations for his drivers. But, in his heart, Ben knew better. His roots were here, in this sprawling little cattle town that looked like a thousand others he had ridden into and away from.

Two square blocks in the heart of this town were Ben Anthony's. He had converted a store building, and the town's only blacksmith shop, to his own use. As a courtesy to the men of this range who had once regarded him with casual patronage, his smithy "shoed" the remudas of any spread who requested it, and for a small fee. And all comers could eat at the small restaurant which Ben had bought out and enlarged so that his drivers and his stagecoach passengers could get a square meal, and thus break the four-day trip from San Antonio to Brownsville. Once, when this twisting road had been a *camino real*, or king's highway, and pompous envoys of his Most Catholic Majesty had driven behind troops of armor-clad soldiers, it had taken a week or ten days to reach the city of missions, the Spanish capital of the province of Tejas. But Ben's stages had cut a minimum of three days off that time, and were being urged to make the trip faster and faster.

Passengers were fed here, and could get a room in the two-story frame hotel that was also Ben Anthony's. Ben never thought that he and Marvin Sledge, between them, owned the town, except for Morgan Mann's sprawling general store and the saloon, which was Fatty Lawrence's; but Fatty owed him a bill for whisky, and he could have taken it over if he had wished.

The saloon's financial status was as uncertain as that of Morgan's store. More men lounged there, and now, as Ben stepped inside, a score of men were milling around. They were not customers for the simple reason that they couldn't pay, and it was well for Ben's purse that he did not own the saloon. (The Mexican couple who operated his small restaurant were complaining vigorously against the custom of dropping in for a meal, and then shrugging off payment with a careless "Put it on the cuff.")

Caddo Parker was leaning on the bar, a glass in his hand, an unfriendly grin on his face, as Ben approached.

Ben spoke first. "Morning, Caddo," he said. But there was no enthusiasm in his voice.

"Belly up," gestured Parker.

Ben Anthony did not refuse, but he indicated by his hesitation that he did not relish Caddo as a drinking companion. He tossed off his drink quickly.

"Have another."

"Too early for me," Ben declined.

"Ride all night and you're ready for a drink," shrugged Caddo. "You can drink all day, and still you don't feel like kicking up your heels at sundown." Then, refilling his glass: "I got a load of hides for you, Ben."

"And your bill of sale, I suppose?" Ben demanded.

Two days before, the day after the meeting at Walt Earnest's, he had delivered that ultimatum to Caddo Parker. No more hides would be accepted for shipment without presentation of a bill of sale.

"Sure, sure," Caddo grinned.

The parting of his lips showed a missing front tooth. Once his kind had rustled steers and delivered them on the hoof to shady operators across the Rio Grande—the Rio Bravo as the Mexicans called it. Now it was harder work for them, but less risk. Cattle had to be slaughtered and stripped of hides. This gruesome work called for more men. But more men were available. And there were fewer line riders to fight off.

Even at this early hour, unemployed riders were sitting miserably in the saloon, and in the shade behind Ben's stable. They could ride over the hill and look for work on a different range, but over there it was the same story. There wasn't a ranch anywhere that could keep a string of riders on its pay roll. Some of the men were bitter about their fate, and out to get theirs where they could. Such men made the lives of the Caddo Parkers a little easier, despite the additional complications. But, Ben mused, sweeping the saloon in one glance, perhaps they weren't all wrong.

His eyes came back to Caddo Parker.

"Five hundred hides," gloated Caddo, "from the Dollar Mark. Got a bill of sale right here."

Ben Anthony started. This was Harry Odell's outfit. Harry had announced at the meeting he intended to sell off some culls. But Ben had not expected anything like this. Since when had the Dollar Mark gotten so big that its owner could sell five hundred head in the off season without touching his stockers!

He took the bill of sale and examined it. Harry's writing all right, a scrawl on a dirty sheet of paper with a dull pencil. But it was enough. Men did not carry a desk and clean white paper with them when they went riding. A bill of sale was usually written on a man's knee with the chewed-off stub of a pencil.

"I'll take 'em," Ben said. "Bring 'em over to my yard."

"Already there," Caddo drawled.

"And I guess," Ben said bitingly, "I might as well drop by Sledge's ranch and pick up a load of tallow."

"Dunno about that," Caddo shrugged. "Sledge, he's in the tallow business. I deal in hides. You and Sledge are speaking, ain't you?"

Ben nodded.

"I don't like insinuations, friend," Caddo said softly. "You're running a freight line, ain't you? You make a living pushing mules, not asking questions."

"Sometimes," Ben murmured, "I amuse myself. A man has to have some fun, Caddo. All work and no play makes Jack a dull boy. And I get a kick out of poking my nose into things. Sometimes."

Caddo's beady eyes studied Ben's face. Thus far they had not clashed. They had even done business together. But there had been a quick mutual dislike at first meeting, and as Caddo stayed longer and longer in the Jim Wells country their relations got more and more strained. Any kind of spark would set off a conflagration. Caddo was as ready as Ben, and was the type of man who took life more or less as he found it, and proceeded to shape what there was with his own bare hands.

"There will be more hides pronto," he added, deciding to push the conversation no further. "Some boys are buying for me. Down south."

There was a grin on his face as he added this explanation. Ben did not believe it, and Caddo did not expect him to. He did not care.

"I'll take all you can show a bill of sale for," Ben called back over his shoulder.

He couldn't explain the rage he felt in Caddo Parker's presence. How and where Caddo obtained his hides was no business of his. As it was none of his affair whether the steers melted down to tallow in Sledge's tallow vats came from Caddo's night riding or from the banker's own purchases. Caddo paid in cash for his freighting, and that was all a man was supposed to ask.

Ben went to his wagon yard and ordered Tommy Melvin to load the hides. There was a load in Port Isabel Tommy could pick up for a return trip: leather and case goods for Morgan Mann.

"Deliver them to the store as soon as you get back," ordered Ben. "Never mind about collecting. I'll drop by and see Morgan."

Tommy was a clean-cut freckle-faced lad who did yeoman work for Ben Anthony. The son of a nester who had divided his time between the Earnest and the Odell range, Tommy would have been a line rider or another homesteader had not Ben shown up with his new business and his offer of employment. As it was, he was Ben's most dependable driver. And useful in many other ways. If the business kept growing, mused Ben, he would promote Tommy to assistant manager. The boy deserved it.

A small frame building, once a saloon, was Ben's office. He was his own bookkeeper, though nothing irritated him like a session with his own accounts. He fumbled through his papers until he located the invoice for Morgan's freight. Eight hundred dollars! Then he swiftly calculated with his feet propped up on his pine board desk. He could add better that way. He could safely carry that account, though profits from the wagons had been off this season. Only the stagecoach business had held up.

Then, locking the office behind him with a sigh, Ben Anthony saddled his bay and galloped to Harry Odell's Dollar Mark, a full ten miles of twisting trail that led through the foothills of the Acalupe range, and that four times crossed Chin-chin Creek. His route carried him through the very heart of the valley range, across a section of Walt Earnest's Wide S pasture, through the back of Keith Maitland's spread. Nearing headquarters, he saw smoke rising from the flats to the south and knew Harry and the Dollar Mark crew were branding away from home.

Harry sang out a cheery Hello and relinquished his branding iron as Ben rode into the clear where he and three Mexican vaqueros were working. Ben dismounted and rolled a smoke, all the time eying the work with critical interest. It was, he thought, a sloppy brand. He said so.

"Why don't you give us a jump?" Harry grinned.

"I haven't got that long," Ben answered.

He wished he had more time. It would be pleasant to shrug aside the cares and responsibilities of his stage and freight line and spend several days with the Dollar Mark crew, as he had done before. Harry Odell was not a competent ranchman. His Mexicans loafed on their riding tricks, and their branding was careless.

Ben sighed. This was the life for a man, not dealing with bulky freight and with squeamish stage passengers. Then he recalled why he had come.

"Caddo is shipping out five hundred hides," he said. "Has your bill of sale."

"I sold 'em," Harry nodded. "I've got too much stock, Ben.

And not enough cash. Dad always did try to overgraze this range."

That was true. But it was strange to hear Harry Odell admit it.

Ben picked up a mesquite stick and began to whittle it into the shape of a pistol. "I don't want to see you get in too deep, podner," he murmured. "You got a nice start. Your dad left you good grass and plenty of stockers. I'd like to see you keep 'em till spring."

"I'm not selling enough to hurt me," Harry protested.

"Plenty of rains lately," added Ben in that same apologetic manner. This country seldom solicited advice, or endured it. "Reckon you can graze more cattle this year than any since '69."

"I'm getting by, Ben," Harry said patiently. "I'm getting by." A queer grin was playing around his mouth.

Yes, he was getting by. Ambition is not always born in a man; sometimes it comes later, of a sudden, of an inspiration. This man who was Harry Odell was considered by his neighbors to be amiable and honest, but without the grim ambition and the stead-fastness to his duties that kept one brand going where others failed. Walt Earnest deplored his daughter's choice because he considered Harry too easy-going. "Why," he had once snorted, "he ain't got an ounce of cattle sense in his whole carcass." Walt had expressed the wish that Harry had more of Ben Anthony's "get up and go."

There had been no reformation. There had been no change, on the surface. Harry Odell was still a good-looking man with a yen for flashy clothes, even in his work, and with a taste for liquor and easy living. But he had changed in these two years, although his neighbors, his future father-in-law, Ben Anthony who was his best friend, did not see this transformation because they were so sure their earlier judgment was right, and final.

"I don't want you on a shoestring," Ben added. "My money ain't good for anything but to help my friends along. Would a couple of thousand do you any good, Harry?"

A refusal was on the tip of Harry Odell's tongue. Then he realized that it would do no harm to accept this loan. Already money was tight. It would get tighter. When he went on spending for his clothes and his whisky, as he intended to do, tongues would wag. It suddenly occurred to him that Ben Anthony was offering him what he needed, an alibi for his unexplainable prosperity. He could offer the explanation that Ben was staking him. The valley would believe that, knowing Ben and knowing Harry. They would know that Ben would make the offer, and that Harry Odell was not one to look a gift horse in the mouth.

"Well, podner," grinned Harry, "I won't turn it down."

Harry had the kind of grin which warmed a heart, male or female. "I could get by," he added, "and I'm not asking you for help. But you know old Harry. Always picking the easy trail. I got some expensive habits, Ben. I'll take your money."

"Fine," Ben nodded. "I can't think of any better use for it. I'll tell Sledge to credit you with two grand. If you get in a jam, come to me for more."

"I'm in no jam now," Harry answered truthfully. He did not bother to explain just how well off he was. "I'm just taking it because I know you won't sleep until I do."

"You're right there," Ben admitted. There had been little affection in his life. One man had loved him as a boy, Walt Earnest, and Walt had never believed in coddling a youngster. Even with his help, Ben had stood on his own feet, forced into taking care of himself. Harry Odell represented to Ben what he had never possessed, boyish wavering undependability and a trusting helplessness.

He stood up, his eyes still avidly watching the brand crew. Any blind man, he wanted to snap out, could make a dollar sign better than that. But Harry Odell did not seem to care, and it was no affair of Ben's. But again he yearned for grass of his own, and riders of his own. None of his own men would ever slap on such a sloppy brand.

"I'll mosey," he said jerkily.

"Come out for a day or two," Harry proposed. "We haven't been hunting in a long time."

"That's right," Ben admitted, his eyes leaping involuntarily to the blue-fringed hills. The deer in those uplands were big and wild. Most men killed their deer in the flats in the early hours of a chill morning. He scorned this easy way of slaying game. In the hills, in the clear of day, the deer had a fighting chance. "I'll be out soon," he promised.

The big man skirted the twisting creek, finally splashing his bay across shallow listless water, and cut deeper into Walt Earnest's pasture. It was out of his way, but since when did a man like him fume at moments spent in riding across hills he knew and loved? A calf caught his eye; Ben unwound his rope and trapped the wide-eyed beast with a quick throw. Sharp thorns had left two jagged cuts across the calf's rump, and both wounds had festered. He took turpentine from his saddle bags and treated the wounds.

A freighter and a stagecoach owner had absolutely no use for turpentine, but Ben was never without it.

There were no horse tracks along the cattle paths. Evidently Walt's range had not been ridden since the last rain, five days before. Ben doubled back and forth several times, on the alert for an ailing calf, studying the Wide S cattle. He was surprised at their fewness; he hadn't realized how Walt was stricken.

Behind him, quickly losing interest in the branding, Harry Odell thought about Ben's loan, and chuckled. Ben had offered it in sympathy, lending a strong shoulder to a friend who had inborn weaknesses. Like Walt Earnest, he felt it a personal concern to see that Harry's backbone did not wilt in these hard times.

Harry Odell enjoyed this picture. There was a streak in his make-up that made him relish any deception, especially his own. Let 'em think so. He did not possess their mute dogged drive in the face of heavy odds, no doubt about it.

"I like the odds with me," he told himself as he left his three vaqueros and rode off without a word of explanation.

His leaving did not affect their work. They were used to being on their own resources as far as care of the Dollar Mark was concerned. They enjoyed this indifference of their employer's. In the first place, they could work at a more leisurely pace; in the second, they could ride together, enjoying animated talk and spicy scandal. Ben Anthony, for instance, would have never let three vaqueros follow the same path; he would have called that a waste of time and men, and sent each one an individual way.

Harry rode slowly across the creek and toward the quick-dropping canyon etched out of these lowlands by the floods of a million years. He left the trail once to ride around a clearing at the mouth of Potter's Spring, where once, legend had it, a man named Potter had been scalped by Indians. And his eyes shone in anticipation as he forgot about Ben Anthony and his own shrewdness in accepting a two-thousand-dollar loan, to speculate on this secret errand. Of late it was becoming more and more difficult to arrange secret meetings with Melba Melvin. Perhaps old Timothy, who lived in that clearing he had so carefully skirted, was getting suspicious. Harry Odell knew he was playing with fire, but, in spite of what this country thought of him, he liked that feeling of experiment and risk, and the thrill of a rendezvous. What this country didn't know, and would never concede, was that a smooth genial man could be as daring, and as dangerous, as a rugged bull-like creature.

Of the three men who had leagued together to make this valley their own—Marvin Sledge, Harry Odell, and Caddo Parker—Parker was regarded as the most dangerous. He shot his way into trouble, and out of it. Sledge and Odell were physical cowards, certainly Sledge. Yet both had dared more than Parker, who was risking only his life, which was cheap to him. Disclosure of their alliance would wreck Sledge and Odell, who had material property and respectability to forfeit.

Harry Odell left the creek bank as it dipped lower and lower toward Dead End Canyon, keeping in the timber, following a dim trail that led to a small cabin perched on a scowling ledge over the chasm. This was Wide S range, but Walt Earnest had used neither the canyon nor the cabin in a long time. The canyon was rough range and more trouble to work than it was worth. When cattle brought high prices he could throw steers in here, hire extra help and come out. But not now. Harry tethered his horse on the ridge to keep it from being seen across the canyon and slipped down the footpath.

Melba would be waiting there as she had promised, he was sure of that. He recalled with a chuckle their first meeting, and then her first surrender. At that, it hadn't taken him as long as he had first figured.

There was no other horse in sight, but this shack, built against the cliff face, was inaccessible on horseback from below. Harry Odell saw that the door was open, and his whistle was gay and tuneful, and his dark eyes danced in anticipation. Melba was cute and sweet. Perhaps too chubby; but he wasn't marrying her,

24

and he needn't worry about her getting fat and coarse with middle age, as most nester girls did. He was marrying Bess Earnest. Melba was just a diversion until then.

He stepped through the door with a light remark, expecting to have Melba come running into his arms in that breathless way of hers. Instead, in the half-gloom, she stood across the cabin, her back to him.

The ejaculation died on Harry Odell's lips as he saw the reason for Melba's refusal to even face him.

There on the rough board bunk, his face a gray shadow in the poor light, but still unmistakable in its determination, sat Timothy Melvin! And the significance of the buffalo gun across his lap was as plain.

For a moment Harry didn't speak. In that moment guilt was written plainly on his face, if he had ever had any intention of denying it. Then his lips moved, and it was typical of him that he spoke in what was an effort at his usual affability.

"Howdy, Timothy."

His face was pale, however. He could utter this casual greeting, and could even recover some of his composure and give Melba a grin and look back to her father with calmness; but he knew there would be nothing casual about this. Although a nester, Timothy Melvin would not grovel before a ranchman, accepting even his daughter's seduction as a part of the harsh fate that was due his kind. He was neither shiftless nor subdued. He worked his land in harmony with the man who owned it, and he held up his head among a breed of men who thought nesters should be beaten down and then driven out. Timothy Melvin, to this Chin-chin valley, wasn't another homesteader, though no man could have expressed the difference.

For a long time Timothy did not speak. Melba turned once, for a pleading look, and then hid her face again.

"This is a hard situation to face, Odell," her father said finally.

This nester had received some formal education, and perhaps read more books even yet than the men who ran cattle on the ranges around him, and who looked down upon him because he worked the ground with his hands.

"Yes, Tim," Harry Odell agreed gratefully. This issue had not been avoided, but he had gained at least a moment's respite.

"If you wasn't a man already spoken," went on Timothy, "it would be easy. I guess Melba should have shown better sense, but she has been a flighty lass ever since she was knee-high to a calf. I've been fearing something like this a long time. I've kept her away from dances in town and I've never let her go to Port Isabel or San Antone with her brother like she's begged. But you, Odell! Your common judgment ought to have stopped you even if Melba was willing from the start. Which she denies she was."

Harry's lips curled, and he shot the girl a quick look of denial. Yes, there had been a small chase. There always had to be. A woman liked to lead a man on, and then of a sudden push him back and reproach him for what had already been done—yet with that reproach to promise other things, in the future that a woman liked to make seem dim and remote, and that a man wanted to be no further away than the next horizon, if not actually at hand.

He didn't answer Timothy Melvin's accusation, not in words. And, perhaps, in the semi-gloom, the nester didn't see his face. Or perhaps he saw, and wished to ignore. He, after all, was her father.

"I don't like this, Odell," Melvin went on. "You're a ranching man, and I know your kind of folks look down on the likes of me and mine. I don't think you should marry up with a girl like Melba any more than she should run off with a greaser vaquero. But I got her to think of. She is a ruined woman. Nobody is gonna take what you throw off. I never thought I would hold a gun on a man and tell him he hasta marry my daughter. Seems to me that's a blamed poor way of starting off married life. But what else is there for me to do, Odell?"

"I don't know." For the moment Harry Odell's mind was absolutely blank. His movements, and his grin, were quick; but his brain worked slowly except in deciding upon his own pleasures. Life had been too easy to stir his mental powers. When there was a break in the even tenor of his existence he was angry, and inclined to sulk.

"I know it upsets your plans, Odell," Timothy Melvin said harshly, but with sorrow in his eyes. "You figgered on marrying well—Walt Earnest's daughter. But you took my girl first—in sin. I hate to throw a choice like this in your lap. But you made your bed, Orell, and you can lie on it."

26

He stood up and gripped his buffalo gun tighter. "You can marry my gal, Harry," he said hoarsely, "or I'll blow your head off."

"Of course I'll marry Melba," Harry Odell said quickly.

He answered too quickly. This wasn't what he had intended to promise at all. It wasn't what he had intended to do. Even in this moment of physical fear, he had no intention of going through with such a ceremony. But he must stall. He was in a corner, and first he must maneuver out of it. Give him time, and he could find a way out.

"I see your side, Tim," he said smoothly. He sat down on the bunk beside the nester and rolled a smoke. He looked down at his fingers and was proud that they didn't quiver. "We lost our heads, both of us. I'm willing to do the right thing. She isn't a wild girl. She'll make a good wife. Give me a little time and—"

"What do you mean by 'time'?" Timothy Melvin demanded, still suspicious.

"Just that," Harry answered, in full possession again of his affable persuasiveness. "I can't just ride into town with you and Melba and get hitched. I got to break off from Bess Earnest gentle-like. We don't want it known over the valley that this was a shotgun wedding. Is there any reason for getting in a hell-fired hurry?"

Timothy Melvin hesitated. Then he turned to his daughter, and his wrinkled face reddened with embarrassment. "Is there?" he asked quietly.

Melba showed them her face for the first time. What was written there was difficult to read. Perhaps it was happiness, but, if so, it was a strange happiness. Standing with her face to the wall, looking away from these two men and yet hearing their every word, she was speculating for the first time upon what it would be like to be married to Harry Odell. She had never considered this. Even when her father had learned of their clandestine affair, and had voiced his determination to kill the handsome ranchman if he would not marry her, Melba had not thought of having Harry as a husband. She knew how stubborn he was in spite of his amiable surface. She hadn't believed that he would yield to her father so easily.

"No," she said in a low voice. "There is no call to hurry."

Her wide eyes appealed to Harry in a sudden change of spirit. She *had* to answer that accusal in his glance.

"Pa followed us last night," she whimpered. "He got me home and made me tell. I didn't want to. He made me."

Harry Odell's eyelids flickered. Damn the nosy old squatter for trailing after them! But he couldn't show his anger. For the moment he was obsessed with the necessity of stalling for time.

"I'll start breaking off with the Earnests right away," he said with dignity. "Say in a month, Timothy, we'll let the word get out that I'm marrying Melba."

"I don't like it, Odell," the nester demurred.

"Can we start married life like this?" demanded Harry, now sure of victory. "Is that the way you want your daughter to have—a wedding that will start a scandal?"

"No," Timothy Melvin reluctantly agreed.

"Then let me handle it. I'm going to marry Melba; but not today, and not with you holding a buffalo gun in front of me. She wasn't my first choice of a wife, but I got no complaints. We'll do this up right, Timothy."

The homesteader let his buffalo gun drop to the dirt floor.

"I'm tickled that you're taking such an attitude, Odell," he said in obvious relief.

"It's the only attitude to take," shrugged Harry.

"Melba can't bring you what Elizabeth Earnest could," muttered the homesteader. "But she'll make you a good wife. She's got a lot of her mother about her. You'll be happy with her, Odell."

"Sure." The ranchman glanced outside. "I gotta ride," he said. "It's almost dark."

Melba Melvin ran across the cabin to him, clutching his arm.

"Harry, it ain't my fault," she pleaded. "Don't be mad at me. I didn't want it this way."

She could be a very pretty girl, for hers was a face that could stand to show emotion. The reckless spirit within Harry Odell, that other men, even a close friend like Ben Anthony, had never discovered, temporarily engulfed the anger and sulkiness at being discovered in a trap of his own setting. He reached down and kissed her cheek lightly.

"I could do worse," he said cheerfully.

That little byplay completely satisfied the bearded nester. He took his daughter's arm.

"We'll walk on back," he said. "Come and see us, Harry. A visit or two would hold back the talk when it starts."

"Sure thing," Harry agreed.

There was nothing about his face that showed he was upset by this unexpected bargain. He watched Melba and her father scramble down the ledge and take the narrow twisting path along the canyon to the spring-fed clearing where the nester had lived these twenty years, with the full approval of Walt Earnest. Then, when they were out of sight, he sat down on the bunk and cursed. How could this happen to him! Melba Melvin wasn't the first conquest he had made among the valley's women. But nothing had come out of the other episodes except the gratification of his own whims.

Now he was faced with the grim reality of reaping what he had sown. Timothy Melvin would carry out his threat, unless Harry killed him. He considered this a moment. No qualm of conscience made him dismiss this alternative. It was fear of punishment. The law would not uphold such a killing, whereas the girl's father could shoot him down with the buffalo gun and any Jim Wells jury would set him free.

Either way, Harry Odell would lose.

The easier decision was to shrug off the idea of marrying Bess Earnest and take Melba as his wife. The nester's daughter was pretty enough, and amusing enough. She would work hard in his house and would probably develop a culinary skill Bess Earnest could never attain. As far as the respective women were concerned, there wasn't enough difference to justify the risk. He had never been anything but cold-blooded about his courtship of Bess Earnest. He had never even felt about Walt's daughter the wild reckless desire he had for other valley girls, including Melba. Bess was desirable as a wife for many reasons. Harry, spoiled to his own narrow point of view, couldn't appreciate the illogical difference that most men find in women when they come to select a wife. Bess was pretty, and, while he deplored her coldness, he had held out this very defect as a task he would enjoy remedying. He anticipated with relish teaching her what it means to a woman to be possessed by a man.

But, more than these things, even more than the impersonal admiration he felt for Bess, was the monetary consideration involved, and the prestige. The merger of the Wide S and the Dollar Mark would give Harry Odell the biggest ranch in South Texas. This handsome man that Walt Earnest and Ben Anthony, who should have known him better than anyone, thought lacking in ambition and initiative had embarked upon a deliberate scheme. He would be the cattle king of this Chin-chin basin. He would even push his herds across the blue-topped hills into the Duval brakes. But it was not love of land or cattle, nor even monetary ambition, that had aroused him to this goal, it was vanity.

One thing had been denied to Harry in his lifetime, and that was the admiration of the boys and men around him. This Ben Anthony had without asking. This Harry must scheme, and work in devious ways, to acquire.

His campaign was already mapped out. He would acquire possession of the Maitland or Cameron spread, if not both, before this panic broke. Marvin Sledge would surely demand one as the banker's share, especially since Harry's marriage to Bess Earnest would add the Wide S to the Dollar Mark when Walt died. Then he would have only Sledge to deal with. And it would have surprised the banker as much as anyone to realize that Harry Odell was perfectly confident of his ability to match wits and cunning with him when that time came.

For Sledge, like Caddo Parker, considered Harry Odell only as a necessary pawn. It simplified their shipping of hides and tallow to have bills of sale for their steers. Parker did not drive his stolen herds out of the valley, nor did he and his night riders even steal in large single quantities. There was, however, a steady dribbling of cattle from the Maitland, Cameron and Earnest ranges onto Dollar Mark grass, and then into the hands of Sledge.

For this Harry Odell received his share. It was a generous share. Sledge and Parker had begrudgingly jacked up his ante. Neither the banker nor the outlaw realized he had outargued them, had even outbluffed them. Scornfully they had granted him a full fourth, then had dismissed him from their serious thoughts. Sledge agreed to a forced purchase of the Maitland outfit because he could never use it himself.

Harry had concealed from his two confederates not only his own astuteness, but his actual profits out of their transactions. Not all of the cattle driven onto the Dollar Mark range by Caddo Parker's men went to Sledge's tallow vats. The ranchman had built up his herd until he was dangerously near to being over-stocked. He had held out from his two cronies something like two thousand head.

It pleased him that neither ever bothered to suspect him. Caddo and Sledge were at each other's throats constantly, each quick to charge the other with falsification. While Harry Odell, the most dangerous of the three, the most far-reaching in his ambition, watched quietly and gloatingly.

He had worked out every detail of his campaign. Except for this—Timothy Melvin's ultimatum. He swore softly as he turned in at his front gate. He could see no way out except to marry Melba Melvin.

But that he had no intention of doing!

Timothy Melvin was a fool if he thought Harry Odell would give up the Wide S, and calm-eyed Bess Earnest, just to appease a nester's wounded pride.

3

WALT EARNEST handed his daughter from the buckboard with the gallantry of a Southern colonel. Then, with a tug at his mustaches, he indicated the saloon with a nod.

"I'll drop over for a drink," he said lamely. "Might bump into Maitland or Cameron."

Elizabeth frowned. It was obvious that none of the Maitlands or Camerons were in Fatty's. None of the horses hitched to the rank bore identifying brands.

"Don't drink much, Dad," she begged.

"I won't, gal," he promised with a sigh. Only Walt Earnest, his daughter, and a San Antonio physician knew of Walt's ailing heart. "A fluttering heart," the physician called it. It could be dangerous if a man of Walt's age would not remember that age.

But his daughter watched with pride the straightness of his walk, the tilt of his white head. Though in the saddle a lifetime Walt Earnest's legs were not bowed; he still had the carriage of an Army officer. When he disappeared into Fatty's she turned to Morgan Mann's general store. Morgan himself met her at the door, and they exchanged pleasantries.

A storekeeper knows the private lives of his people as well as their hearts. It did not miss Morgan's attention that in Ben Anthony's blacksmithy the ringing of a hammer suddenly came to a halt, and that in a moment Ben came out wringing-wet with perspiration and walked to his small office.

By now Elizabeth was examining bolts of dress goods Morgan had just received from Port Isabel.

"I'd bet a drink," he murmured in a soft voice, to no one in particular, "that Anthony changes his shirt and just remembers that he forgot to buy something over here."

32

Morgan turned to his customer. "That brocade there is prime stuff," he suggested. He was not a storekeeper who pushed his wares upon his customers. Everything was there where they could see; let 'em pick out what they wanted.

"We need new curtains," Elizabeth said, her lips forming an O of indecision. "But we also need groceries. I'm afraid we owe you too much to buy things like curtains."

"Oh, not so much," Morgan said carelessly.

"How much, Morgan?"

"Oh, I dunno. I don't figger on what people owe me every day of the world. Sledge now, he can tell you right to a penny what the amount of your loan is, including the interest. But I don't rightly know, Bessie."

"I'd like to know," she gently insisted. "You know Dad—he's never worried about a dollar in his life. We're going to have to do some figuring out at the Wide S to get by. It's up to me to do some calculating."

Morgan nodded and went to his desk. He studied some entries in his big black-bound book, then returned.

"A mite over nine hundred dollars," he said.

"Morgan! You know we owe more than that. We haven't paid you in two years."

"Gal, I've been adding up accounts for twenty years," grinned Morgan. "Nobody ain't ever accused me of undercharging 'em before. Usually it's the other way around."

"I'm sure there is something wrong," Elizabeth accused him.

Morgan's face showed unimpeachable innocence. "That's what the bill is," he shrugged.

Now the storekeeper was grinning. Sure enough, there was Ben Anthony coming across the street in a clean shirt.

"Howdy, Ben," he drawled.

"Howdy, Morgan. Got a small notebook and a new pencil?"

"Sure, sure," Mann agreed, turning to his shelves.

"Howdy, Ben."

"Howdy, Bess. How come the Wide S in town today?"

"Walt was itching. Isn't this pretty material, Ben? I could re-cover our living-room chairs and make new curtains out of this and—"

"Change the whole room plumb around," Ben grinned. "You

were doing that when you were a gal in pigtails. I can remember staying out with the cattle all night so I wouldn't have to push furniture around."

Elizabeth laughed. "We sure overworked you. You never had a chance to grow up, did you?"

"How's Walt?"

"Oh, grouchy as ever."

He studied her calm face. "The San Antone doctor," he said gently, "isn't so sure. Better make him take it easy, Bess."

"How did you know that?" Elizabeth asked sharply.

"I got drivers in San Antone," he shrugged. "They saw Walt going to this doctor. I can put two and two together, Bess."

"I'm worried, Ben. So is he. He wants me to rush the wedding. He says he'll feel better, knowing I'm settled."

A shadow flitted across Ben's face. This was the handicap he always faced with Bess Earnest. Out of loyalty to Harry Odell, his friend, he couldn't say what he felt.

"Sure," he agreed. "Harry is getting sharper with cattle. He could take some of the load of the Wide S off Walt."

"No one will ever do that in Dad's lifetime," Bess sighed. "But I know it would make Dad feel better to know it's all settled. I guess we'll set a date pretty quick, Ben."

"That makes sense."

The big man was suddenly uncomfortable. He could never talk long to Bess Earnest without this subject coming up—her approaching marriage to Harry Odell.

"Gotta mosey," he said abruptly. "Write the pencil and book down, Morgan."

"Sure," agreed the storekeeper. He turned his attention to Elizabeth Earnest.

"I can cut the price on that brocade 10 per cent if you want it," he offered.

"Fine. I'll take ten yards, Morgan."

The fleshy storekeeper began to unroll the brocade. "So you're splicing up with Harry?" he asked idly. "Always figgered you and Ben would make a good team."

"Ben!" smiled Elizabeth. "Oh, he's been too much like a brother, Morgan. He's never looked at me twice since I was a spindly-legged girl."

34

"He's doing well," Morgan murmured. "In fact, I guess Ben is a rich man. It ain't worrying him none, and he ain't throwing his weight around, but I guess Ben could buy and sell most of us here in Alice without feeling the strain."

"I wouldn't doubt it," Elizabeth agreed heartily. Too heartily. The trouble was, Morgan sighed as he watched her return to the buckboard and await her father, that Ben had too many virtues for a woman. Or did he have?

"I'd like to see that big waddy cut loose and go on a spree," growled Morgan to himself.

Outside there was a clatter of hoofs, and Harry Odell galloped up. He saw Elizabeth in the buckboard and quickly tethered his horse and joined her. The admiration in his dark eyes brought a flush to the girl's cheeks. Harry had never lacked this power to stir her, not even when they had been boy and girl together.

"And if you're not sweeter-looking than the sage on a frosty morning!" he told her. "Where's Walt?"

"Inside. And I'm afraid he's having too many. Chase him out for me, Harry."

"Me!" he groaned. "Since when did Walt Earnest take orders from me?"

"Tell him I sent you."

"Well, I'll try it," he said hesitantly. He took a step toward the saloon, turned back. "How about receiving company tonight?" he smiled.

"Sure, Harry. For supper?"

"I was hoping you'd ask me," he chuckled.

He shot a look back over his shoulder, and his face hardened. Timothy Melvin must be loco to think a man would pass over a woman like Bess Earnest to marry a homesteader's chubby-cheeked daughter. His lips parted in an unpleasant smile. He thought he had the answer to Melvin's ultimatum.

Inside, Walt Earnest was, as his daughter feared, having his third drink. And the Wide S owner was feeling his liquor. He was addressing the bartender, but his speech was plainly meant for Caddo Parker, who lounged at a corner table idly playing solitaire.

"I had a little more respect for rustlers than I do for these hide strippers," Walt was saying. "Can't blame a man so much for wanting to steal cattle on the hoof. But a hide stripper is the lowest-down son-uvva-gun this side of the Mexican border. I don't know whether he's good enough to associate with greasers—"

"Howdy, Walt," Harry interrupted. "Bess is outside and claims it's time to take off like a sage hen."

"Have a drink, Harry."

"No, better go on. You know Bess when she's kept waiting."

"It ain't often I ride in for a drink," Walt snapped. He turned back to the bar. "Fill 'er up, Fatty," he growled defiantly.

Now Ben Anthony came through the door, shutting off all light for a moment. Walt saw him and barked out a gruff greeting. But neither Harry nor Ben was fooled. The light in Walt's eyes gave him away.

"You overgrown sheep dipper, do you want a drink?" Walt demanded.

"No," Ben said calmly. "Neither do you. Bess is ready to make tracks."

"Damnation," muttered Walt. "A man can't have a drink in peace without a woman's interrupting. Well, no use of getting her fired up. Come out right soon, Ben."

Harry Odell's lips tightened. He was Walt Earnest's future son-in-law. But his admonition not to drink any more had merely inspired the mustached ranchman to another glass. One word from Ben Anthony, and Walt was ready to leave.

"I'll do that," Ben said.

Walt staggered a little.

"Wanna talk to Bess myself," Ben explained. "I'll walk with you." He steadied the old ranchman with a tug.

Harry grinned. If he was to lay a hand on Walt, he'd be knocked flat. He ordered a drink and sipped it slowly. He turned with the glass in his hand and looked at Caddo Parker.

"Howdy, Parker," he said coldly.

This was Caddo Parker's lot, to be spoken to curtly in daylight by men who were his associates by night. He didn't care. He had ridden outside the law for a long time. He had developed an ironic sense of humor.

"Yes, Odell?" he barked back.

"I rode through my lower pasture today, Caddo. I can let you have a hundred head of culls if you want the hides."

"Hides," Caddo said, "is my business."

He laid down his cards. "Wet your whistle while we talk it over," he said, coming to the bar.

"I've had a drink, thanks," Harry Odell said grimly. Such was the way every ranchman treated Caddo Parker, even those who sold hides to him. "Ride out tomorrow, and we'll count 'em out."

"It'll be late, I got to duck over to the Duval country."

"Any time," shrugged Odell. "I'll be home."

Caddo Parker made a barely perceptible nod. The look in the ranchman's eyes indicated that he wanted more of him than to sell a hundred culls for slaughter and skinning. Caddo grinned as Odell left the saloon and walked across the street to the wagon yard. The fellow played a dangerous game, and he played it well. Caddo, who had played for high stakes in all kinds of games, of life and of cards, was beginning to wonder if he and Marvin Sledge had not underestimated Harry Odell.

Caddo lit a cigar and surveyed the furnishings of the house. Harry Odell's father had been more expensive in his tastes than other men just molding this rough country to their own wills. There were upholstered chairs here, and rugs, and pictures.

"A nice layout," Caddo approved.

"It'll do," Harry murmured.

As he held his cigar to the flickering candle and downed the glass of whisky his guest watched with some amusement. The young fellow was plenty worried about something. Caddo Parker had his troubles, but the fear of discovery was not one of them. And never had been. Hard as he was, he had never been guilty of deception.

"What's eating you?" Caddo finally demanded.

"Plenty," Harry said jerkily. "You know Tim Melvin?"

Caddo nodded.

"I played around with his girl. The old coot caught us together and—"

"Pointed his gun at you and told you to ride to town for a license," grinned the outlaw. "That's tough, son. Ol' Timothy will

37

blast the living hell out of you if you don't buy a ring and call a preacher pronto."

"I can't do that," Harry growled. "I'm going to marry Bess Earnest. You know that."

"Sure," shrugged Caddo, who knew more about this man than even Harry had ever guessed. There were two sides to Harry Odell, a bad side and a good side, a weak side and a strong side. Caddo had seen both, hence he could arrive at judgments no other valley man could even touch. "I don't blame you. That Wide S range ain't to be sneezed at."

"Nor the girl," growled Harry, irked that the other could see through him so easily. "I ain't marrying the Melvin wench, Caddo. And I don't want to look down the barrel of Timothy's buffalo gun."

Caddo Parker shrugged his shoulders. This good-looking man, whose sinister side was so cleverly concealed, had an idea. Caddo was coming to have more and more respect for the ranchman's ideas. At first he and Sledge had done the scheming, with Harry Odell only a necessary pawn. Sledge still believed that was their arrangement. Parker, more experienced in such "deals," knew better.

"You can help me out, Caddo," proposed Odell. "And yourself at the same time."

"Mainly," drawled the outlaw, studying the tip of his cigar, "I'm interested in the latter."

"Sure. You want hides, don't you?"

"Bales of 'em," was the prompt answer. "I want so many hides Ben Anthony will have to buy extra wagons to freight 'em to Port Isabel. But what's that got to do with Timothy Melvin? I can't sell *his* hide, Odell. And Sledge wouldn't get a thimbleful of tallow out of that dried-up carcass."

"Here's my idea. Take your boys and run a few head of Walt's stock up the canyon. Slaughter 'em, leave their hides in that cabin just up from Potter's Spring. You know the place, don't you?"

Caddo Parker nodded. He knew this country as well as many ranchmen who had lived here all of their lives. In his business a man did a lot of riding, and noticing.

"Then take some of the hides to Ben Anthony and show him

38

a bill of sale from Timothy Melvin," Odell concluded triumphantly. "That will fix Melvin's goose in this valley. Anthony will report it to Walt. Old Walt will be after Melvin like a mad ant. Walt will chase Melvin off his range and out of the country. Then I won't have to marry the girl."

Caddo closed his eyes a moment, thinking back over what Harry Odell was proposing. His lips parted in a rough grin.

"There are some objections," he murmured. "In the first place, I don't seem to be getting much out of it. Neither does Sledge."

"To hell with Sledge," Harry snorted.

"No," Caddo said firmly, "we're in this together. I ain't much of a hand for a double-cross, Odell."

It was strange that Caddo Parker, the undisguised rider of owl-hoot trails, should have to remind first Marvin Sledge, then Harry Odell, that there was supposed to be honor even among thieves. Of the three, in their dealings with one another, only Parker was capable of generosity.

"It's in line with what Sledge is trying to do," Harry argued. "He wants Walt Earnest whipped down."

"Yes, he does," Caddo murmured. His beady eyes studied Harry. "Since you're gonna latch on to the Wide S when you marry Walt's daughter you oughta be opposing that. Seems like to me a cow stole from the Wide S is a cow stole from you. Or is there an angle I ain't figgered?"

"There is," Harry said curtly. "Walt Earnest thinks I'm a fool. To him Ben Anthony is the paragon of all virtues. He's got an idea I want his cattle and his grass. I want the grass. I can use the cattle. But I'd rather, even if it's the same as money out of my own pocket, have Walt stone-broke by spring."

"So," guessed Caddo, "you can come to his rescue, save the Wide S from foreclosure with your cash, and let the old man know you can carry your own weight."

"That's about it."

"Well, that's straight in my mind." Caddo Parker grinned. "Now, about this Melvin deal. I don't like it, Odell. I got nothing again Timothy. Why should I pull *your* chestnuts out of the fire?"

"If I hafta marry his girl," blazed Harry, piqued that this

rustler could outargue him, "our whole deal is off. The Wide S stays on its feet. Walt Earnest takes over the reins, and you and me and Sledge will be hitting for the timber."

"Oh, no," smiled Parker. "The Wide S goes under. Sledge says so. Mebbe Sledge will take over Walt's range. I dunno but what that ain't Sledge's notion anyhow."

Harry Odell's eyes gleamed. He had anticipated this line of argument. He had an answer ready.

"The Wide S won't go under, Parker," he snapped. "Either I save it, against the day I'll inherit it, or Ben Anthony does."

"Anthony!" This was another angle the owl-hooter hadn't considered.

"That's right," Harry said triumphantly. "You know he will."

"Can he do it?"

"Take my word for it, he can," Harry promised. "He has the chips. Another thing to think about. You don't want Anthony after your hides."

"I dunno. I've been called tough by some."

"Anthony can break you to pieces with his bare hands," Harry asserted. And he meant it. In many ways he had slipped. But his boyhood admiration of Ben Anthony was unchanged. In his heart he sneered at some of the big man's shortcomings. But he was quick to concede, and uphold, Ben's abilities. Especially as a fighter, with either guns or fists.

"Besides," he added, heaving a sigh, "I'll make it worth your while to plant the hides in that cabin. Nobody but Melvin has used it in a long time. Walt will know whom to lay the blame on. I'll pay a thousand cash, Caddo. On the line."

"I could use a thousand," Caddo said slowly. His eyes studied the ranchman's face. "Where do I get the bill of sale from Melvin?" he demanded.

"I'll write it out—right now," Harry proposed, turning to his desk.

"What if he denies it? Melvin, I mean. If it comes to a showdown, will his word be taken against mine?"

"I'll lay a plant," Harry said. "I don't think it will come to a showdown. I know Walt Earnest's temper."

"I don't like it," frowned Caddo. But, even as he deliberated, he knew he would do what this man wanted. He stood up, reluctant to leave this comfort, but sure their business was over.

"It won't backfire," Harry promised.

Caddo regarded his host with a thin smile around his bearded lips.

"You're a slick one," he murmured. "You're also a sorry galoot. You're worse than me, Odell."

Naturally this was a compliment Harry Odell did not relish.

"I don't like it either," he shrugged. "But I'm backed against the wall, Caddo. This is the only way out that I can figger."

Caddo accepted another drink, then rode back toward Alice. For an owl-hooter with a night rider's past, he told himself with a chuckle, he was certainly moving in high company. His next call was upon Marvin Sledge, the banker, to whom he repeated what Odell had proposed.

"The danged fool!" ejaculated Sledge. "What did he have to get himself mixed up with Melvin's girl for!"

"She ain't bad to look at," said Caddo in the ranchman's defense. "I wouldn't mind some complications in that line myself."

"You're different," snapped Sledge. "You're not going to marry Elizabeth Earnest in the spring."

"No," Caddo said with obvious regret, "I ain't."

His sigh indicated that he wouldn't mind substituting for Harry Odell in that direction either.

"I've been afraid of Odell all along," speculated Sledge, drumming on his unpainted desk top. "The damned fool! We were almost ready to take this valley over, then he stops to make love to a nester's gal. I need Odell, Caddo. I got to have him."

"You need a man," Caddo guessed shrewdly, "to take over the Wide S?"

"That's right. Odell is the perfect man."

"You're afraid it will be Ben Anthony."

"You know a lot," growled Sledge.

"I ain't a fool," grinned the outlaw.

"Do you think you can get by with this business?" demanded the banker.

"It ain't my style," shrugged Caddo. "If Timothy Melvin is in the way, what's wrong with dropping him from the brush?"

"That wouldn't get his family out of this country," frowned Sledge. "I guess Odell's plan is the only answer."

"Why?"

"Because," snapped Sledge, "if Melvin was shot down by parties unknown, and it got out that Odell was the man who led his daughter astray, Odell would be pulled in for Tim's murder. And he'd hang for it just as sure as we're sitting here."

"I hadn't thought of that," agreed Caddo.

He stood up with a sigh. He had figgered himself a pretty smart hombre until he had struck this Alice region and had teamed up with Marvin Sledge and Harry Odell. He was learning more about operating from these two than he had ever learned.

"I guess mebbe," he told himself as he swung into his saddle, "I've stepped out of my class."

4

CADDO PARKER rode out to study the layout around the Melvins', even dismounting and climbing up to the abandoned line cabin where Odell had suggested he place the incriminating hides. He looked down at the small cabin where Timothy Melvin had raised his large family against the terrible odds that any nester on a Texas range had to face. He spent a moment wondering why a man like Melvin had stayed here. In other states a nester had the right to file homestead claims, but Texas had retained its public land as a condition of its entering the Union, and the only way to acquire public land was to buy it in large units. Yet on every range Caddo had ever seen there had been nesters clinging with mute stubbornness to cabin sites that could never be theirs. It didn't make sense to him. He preferred his own way of living.

Then, stony-faced, Caddo cut across the slopes toward the Wide S headquarters, sizing up Walt Earnest's pastures. From a wooded ridge he saw how Walt's cattle were drifting down toward the flats; and he decided that the easiest way to cut out a small herd would be to ride in from the ridges and force the steers down into the draw, where, at a drift fence, they could be turned and driven along the creek toward the canyon. There would be plenty of tracks, but in these times Caddo did not have to worry so much about leaving a trail.

He saw Ben Anthony ride up to Walt's gate, where Bess Earnest met him, and he wondered with a crooked grin if Odell was taking too much for granted there. Then he shrugged his shoulders and galloped back to Alice.

Caddo's business was stealing cattle, driving them to Sledge's tallow vats, and then shipping the hides to Isabel. The times were in his favor. He could take his pick of a half-hundred men loafing helplessly about town, and he could pay them just about what he chose. Most of them would have been honest men had they been given a chance. He knew that some of them despised him even as they accepted his orders. But that worried him precious little.

Caddo selected five men, rode with them to a temporary camp pitched behind the shelter of an abandoned corral, and outlined his plans. One man's lips moved in protest. Once he had worked for Walt Earnest. Caddo made a mental note of this rider's objection. The man's name was Pickett. Perhaps something would happen to him on the raid. Men in these times were about as cheap as cattle.

His men gathered in the salt flats behind Chin-chin Creek and waited for the moon to come up. They could wait for the moonlight now, Caddo and his kind. There were no Wide S crews camping out in line cabins to be aroused by their thundering hoofs, and then their pistol fire as they herded the frightened cattle together. Caddo's business had known more profitable times, but not safer ones.

The six riders scattered into the brushy flat, and soon the night was heavy with telltale noises, the grunt and snort of a resentful steer, the clatter of a horse breaking in swift pursuit, the scraping of mesquite thorns against leather chaps. Caddo watched from a ridge, shouting his orders as if these slopes and these cattle belonged to him by law and he had nothing to fear from detection.

By moonlight the night riders closed in their sweep, driving surly bawling cattle ahead. They took the open trail across the ridge toward Sledge's Long S, toward the draw where the dollar-minded Sledge had set up three immense tallow vats. Gruesome things these were, of cast iron with ovens underneath. Mexican hands had piled mesquite wood high here.

Caddo called out orders, and his men began shooting down the bawling steers and working on their carcasses with skinning knives. The stench of rotting flesh and freshly skinned hides was enough to turn the stomach of any man. Roused by the noise, some of Sledge's vaqueros came down from the Long S bunkhouse and joined in the work. The Mexicans were better with the skinning knives than Caddo's recruits from the saloon, and accepted this repulsive work without rancor.

"Why not?" Caddo grunted to one of his riders who commented on the Mexicans' cheerful acceptance of this way of making a living. "Sledge never fed his riders beef before. Now they can help themselves to a quarter any time they choose."

Which was true. The Long S vaqueros claimed half a yearling as their own. Caddo watched them butcher the calf and then ordered breakfast.

"We'll have son-of-a-bitch stew when we finish, boys," he told his men.

The fires were crackling high under the vats when the bleeding carcasses were thrown into them.

"Sledge don't slaughter his own steers," observed Caddo. "Not enough fat on 'em to make tallow."

More complaints from his men. They had punched cattle or stolen cattle all their lives. It didn't seem right to see fresh meat boiling up, and down, and coming out shapeless, tasteless tallow.

"I swam rivers to get sorrier meat than this up the trail," said one of the owl-hooters.

Caddo nodded. He felt much the same way. But where could a man dispose of stolen cattle these days?

The hides stripped, he called a halt. Sledge's Mexicans could finish the rest. From the vaqueros' camp came the appetizing smell of sizzling steak. And tortillas. Caddo's men ate wolfishly. There was no coffee; to this complaint, he snarled, "I ain't running a de-luxe hotel."

He selected twenty of the hides, rolled them in a bale, and tied them behind his saddle. These he would cache at the canyon cabin.

"All right, boys," he ordered. "Let's vamoose."

He turned to the foreman of Sledge's vaqueros. "Bring the rest of them hides to Anthony's wagon yard today," he ordered.

"Bueno."

Caddo rode a half-mile with his riders, then reached out and caught Pickett's bridle. Pickett was the new man who had formerly ridden for Walt Earnest's Wide S.

"Ride up this road with me a spell," he growled.

45

The man followed without a protest.

Caddo pulled up his chestnut a mile from the forking. "Reckon you're too friendly with Walt Earnest to suit me, Pickett," he said coldly.

"What do you mean? I worked for Walt a spell. He treated me white. I got nothing agin him."

"Sure. And you don't like stealing from your old boss."

Now Pickett's voice showed fear. "Caddo, what's eating you? You ain't afraid of me squealing, are you?"

"That's right," Caddo Parker answered in a dull monotone. Once he would have minded a bit of business like this. But a man got used to it in time. It became just part of a night's work, and a man like Caddo just shrugged it off as an unpleasant but necessary chore.

With a curse the rider clawed for his gun. Caddo shot first. It wasn't a fair fight. He had his hand on his gun when Pickett started his draw. He had come prepared, Pickett was taken by surprise.

But men like Caddo, who have night-ridden a long time, can't give every passing rider a fair chance. The odds would sooner or later be against him. If a man stayed alive, he had to turn them into his favor. They were heavy enough already without any gestures toward gallantry.

The rider slumped from his saddle with a groan. His well trained horse stood placid, staring down at the fallen man in mild surprise. Caddo seized the bridle and rejoined his men.

There was no comment. Several eyed the riderless horse with questioning eyes and with sudden catches in their throats. But none voiced an inquiry.

It was daylight when they reached the Wide S forking again. Caddo sent the other four riders on into town, ordering them to grab some sleep and meet him at Fatty's later in the day. He took his bale of hides and rode the back trail toward the canyon, skirting high in the timber above the small house that housed Timothy Melvin and his family.

Reaching the line cabin, Caddo tossed the hides into a corner, making no effort to conceal them. He eyed them grimly. Would Walt Earnest fall for such a fool plant? Probably so. Cattlemen's blood ran hot at this rustling and slaughtering, hotter than even

46

at rustling alone. They would leap at the chance to wreak vengeance upon a lone culprit.

Anyhow, shrugged Caddo, he had done his job. He could collect his thousand from Harry Odell.

He rode into town at a gallop, sleepy and hungry. He stopped at the saloon for three swift drinks, then went to Ben Anthony's restaurant.

Ben was also eating. The big man gave him a cold stare, then turned back to his scrambled eggs. When he had finished, he strode over to Caddo's table.

"Reckon you can grab your grub somewhere else, Caddo," he growled.

"Ain't this a public restaurant?" the outlaw asked unblinkingly.

"No. It's for stagecoach passengers. Alice people are welcome to trade here, most of 'em. You're not."

Caddo Parker's eyelids flickered. Sledge and Odell were always warning against trouble with this big gray-eyed man. But that trouble had to come. Nobody had ever pushed Caddo around like this.

"I might stay out, Anthony," he said slowly, "and I might not. There ain't another restaurant in this town. When I get hungry, I like to eat."

"I've warned you," Ben Anthony shrugged. "I don't want you trading here. We don't need your money."

"I got some hides to ship," Caddo murmured. "Mebbe you don't want them either."

"I'll take 'em if you show a bill of sale."

"I always got a bill of sale, Anthony," drawled Caddo. He stood up and tossed a silver dollar onto the counter. "Give the change to Anthony here," he jeered.

He looked at Ben, and his lips parted in a coarse smile. "Sometimes, Anthony," he murmured, "you act as if you think I'm a crook."

Walt Earnest was up early. Now, with no crew of riders, it was his job to feed the string of horses before breakfast. He rubbed down his favorite mount, a sleek paint which Ben Anthony had broken six years before, and was feeding the horse oats when Bess called from the house that breakfast was ready.

Until the last year there had been a trio of Mexican women who did the household chores, leaving Walt's motherless daughter to live the life of a lady. But now she was cook, housekeeper, and even Walt's assistant at riding the broad ranges. Sometimes she even applied turpentine to a stricken calf's thorn scratches while her father held it.

Walt ate in grim silence, then pushed back his plate. He was troubled, Bess sensed that. Of late he seldom smiled.

"Anything on your mind, Dad?" she asked.

"Plenty," he snapped. "We're losing cattle. There ain't an unbranded calf or cow in the flats. I rode through there yesterday."

Ordinarily this would not be startling news to Bess Earnest. The flats were common grasslands, with Maitland and Cameron and Odell stock gradually working toward the creek in a dry season. But none of the three outfits had staged a spring roundup. Only Harry Odell had riders going into the flats with branding irons. Maitland, Alan Cameron, and Walt had agreed to let the cows run together, and to stage a community roundup when they had the riders to work the brush.

"Not a maverick," grumbled Walt. "It doesn't make sense."

"It should come as no surprise to you," Bess pointed out. "Caddo Parker and his men make a living somehow. And Marvin Sledge keeps shipping out tallow."

"Sledge claims he is foreclosing on outfits all of the time," Walt pointed out. "Says when he takes an outfit over he has to strip the hides and boil the carcasses into tallow to get anything out of the foreclosure. I wouldn't say Sledge is helping Parker steal cattle."

"I would," said Bess with a toss of her head.

"But Caddo ain't getting *all* of the unbranded stock," Walt said grimly.

"Who else? You wouldn't accuse Maitland? Or Alan? Not after they gave you their word."

In other years it had been a race to see who slapped brands on mavericks. Most seasons found Walt and his Wide S crew getting into the flats first, and thereby annexing the major portion of the unbranded young stock. Several times, their disputes over ownership of these mavericks had resulted in gunfire. But Walt was loath to believe that either Maitland or Cameron would break his given word. They had been his range enemies, and their armistice was only a temporary thing; but still he respected them. He glared at Bess and stomped out of the room. Was she a danged fool! Hadn't he told her as plain as day that he suspected Harry Odell of slapping brands on everything in the flats! The day hadn't come when that was considered dishonest. But it was, growled Walt to himself, jumping on a man who was flat on the ground.

"I can help you this afternoon, Dad," Bess volunteered as he pulled on his shapeless work hat.

"All right," he said glumly. He was still thinking about Harry Odell. "Wasn't Ben here yesterday?" he asked after a moment.

"Yes, he was."

"Fine boy," Walt said heartily. "They don't come any finer than Ben."

"They sure don't," Bess replied with an enthusiasm which matched his own.

Walt sighed. That was the trouble. Bess was crazy about Ben. But she didn't realize it. She thought of him as a big brother, and couldn't for the life of her see the look in the big man's eyes, which wasn't brotherlike at all. If Ben would speak, if he would shock the living daylights out of her with his declaration and set her to thinking, set her to comparing Ben Anthony with Harry Odell, then Odell wouldn't have a chance. Walt Earnest had that much confidence in his daughter's judgment. But until she got rid of this brother-sister notion, Odell was top man. And the time was pushing close.

Walt picked up his rifle and swung stiffly into the saddle. He couldn't keep up this riding much longer. Several times each day he had to stop and rest. If Bess ever caught him at it, she would make him give up riding altogether, in spite of what would happen to their cattle. His blood pressure was getting higher and higher; he didn't have to pay the San Antonio doctor another visit to realize that. But to abandon the Wide S, to let a man like Caddo Parker take over this range . . . He'd ride himself to death first.

He circled the upper pasture and regarded the yearlings grazing around the natural tank thrown up by interwoven ridges. Walt Earnest was ahead of his time in building up his stock.

Wild longhorns ran in the flats, but the Wide S stock in these close pastures were near-Herefords and Durhams. These yearlings were worth twice as much per pound as longhorns—in normal years, that is. They weren't trail cattle, but Walt had abandoned the idea of trailing north, preferring to ship by boat to New Orleans and Mississippi River markets. That called for a better type of dressed cow. A longhorn cost as much to ship as a Hereford. In fact, more.

But now, wild longhorns and near-blooded beef alike were worth no more than their tallow weight and their hides.

Walt turned his horse toward the flats. It was brushier here, and it would be good business for him and the Maitlands and the Camerons to continue their armistice as far as this low country was concerned. Took a heap of hands to round up steers here. Throwing their outfits together, splitting the mavericks among 'em, they could save cost. And no good beef came out of this brush. No blooded calf could feed here, and the longhorns were rail-thin even in the spring.

Chin-chin Creek parted the thickets momentarily, but only so. Walt splashed across it, no more than a ripple of muddy water, and there found the first signs of Caddo Parker's raid.

He dismounted for a study of their tracks. Six riders. That eliminated Harry Odell and his three vaqueros, who had a right in here along with the Maitlands and the Camerons. Walt climbed back into his saddle and gripped the butt of his rifle. The tracks had been made last night.

The trail was easy to follow. Walt even found where Caddo Parker had sat his horse on the ridge top, directing the movements of his men like a general. He saw the zig-zagging trail to the deeper flat, where Chin-chin Creek widened, and then where the milling steers were swept together by the point men and started up the trail toward the ridge road.

This road led toward Falfurrias. Walt followed for several miles. The trail turning off to Marvin Sledge's was chopped up, but so was the fork coming in from Falfurrias. He couldn't tell whether his cattle had been driven on up the Falfurrias road or turned into Sledge's.

He brooded a moment. He didn't like the banker, but one couldn't hurl accusations against a man simply because of a personal dislike. He rode slowly toward Sledge's headquarters. He sighted the vaqueros working at the vats and pulled up to give the gruesome objects a disgusted study. It was his first sight of Sledge's vats.

The fires underneath were burning out. The Mexicans were rolling the hardening tallow into bales.

Walt dismounted and stalked forward.

"Coma sta," he said awkwardly. His Spanish was always poor. Younger men in this country picked up Mexican as if they were born to it. Men of Walt's generation would never learn. He had seldom hired Mexican riders.

"Bueno," Sledge's foreman answered curtly. He pretended to be unable to speak English, but he understood it all right. He understood, too, why Walt Earnest had ridden up.

Walt searched his meager Spanish vocabulary. No, he didn't have the words to ask his questions. He turned, and with gestures, indicated that he wanted to see the hides. The Mexican foreman nodded and waved him on to the wooden shack where steer hides were packed head-high, awaiting one of Ben Anthony's wagons to carry them to Port Isabel.

Walt did not find a Wide S brand on any hide. There were several carrying Maitland's Short Rail, but he had no intention of kicking up a stink about that. A few cattle didn't matter. Marvin Sledge was probably unaware that any Short Rail steers had been gathered in. The others were all Marvin's or of foreign brands.

He came back to the Mexican foreman, murmured "Buenos días," and rode on back to his range. He sighted Keith Maitland against the sky line and fired his revolver to attract attention. Maitland waited, and swore softly when Walt announced that some eighty of his beeves had been driven off the night before.

"Lost their track on the Falfurrias road," grunted Walt. "Sledge has driven in so danged many cattle from Duval County that you can't tell nothing."

"Where would they be driving 'em to, except to Sledge's?" demanded Maitland, rolling a cigarette. "Sure they didn't double back on you, Walt?"

"I didn't look too close."

"Let's pick up Rex and ride a fan," proposed Keith, referring to his brother.

The trio rode the Falfurrias trail back and forth, on the alert for evidence that a herd had been turned off and driven back toward Sledge's vats. There were no such signs.

"Could they have been driven straight to Sledge's?" asked Rex Maitland.

"None of my hides there," grunted Walt.

"You don't reckon they could already be in town?"

Walt shook his mustaches vigorously. "That's worth a try," he conceded. "Ben said he wouldn't take any hides for shipping from Caddo Parker without a bill of sale."

"How many of 'em were unbranded, Walt?" Keith asked.

"No telling," sighed the Wide S owner. "But not over twenty, I'd guess. I'll ride in and see Ben."

"We'll go along," said Keith. "Need to pick up some tobacco anyhow."

The trio rode in grim silence into Alice. They found Ben Anthony just supervising the loading of the Corpus-bound wagon that carried Caddo's hides.

"Ben, a word with you?" Walt Earnest called out.

Anthony left the wagon and joined them at the gate.

"Sure, Walt. What's eating you?"

"See you got some hides there?"

"Yes."

"Caddo?"

"Yes."

"Reckon any of 'em have a Wide S brand on 'em?"

"Why? You hit last night?"

"About eighty head."

"About sixty here. That's Caddo's count."

"What brand they carry?"

"Those on top and bottom carry no brand," Ben said. "Some on the inside might—I dunno. Caddo showed me a bill of sale, that's all I asked."

"Mind if we look?" Walt asked grimly, dismounting.

"Go ahead," Ben shrugged. "Only you got to tie the hides up again when you get through."

He helped the ranchman unroll the bundle. Walt's white

mustaches quivered as he pointed to several Wide S markings. "Thought you were watching out for me, Ben?" he croaked.

"I didn't tear the bundle open," apologized Ben. "Tim Melvin signed the bill of sale, and I figgered—"

"Melvin!" snorted Walt. "Since when has he any cattle to run?"

"He had a small spread once," claimed Ben. "When I rode for you. We used to brand 'em for him."

"Sure, I was helping him out. But I bought up his stuff two years ago. Lost money on 'em too."

"I didn't know that," Ben said slowly. "I figgered he still had some."

"Show me the bill of sale," Walt demanded suspiciously.

Ben produced the rough document given to him by Caddo Parker. The bill of sale on dirty paper, pencil-written. Walt made out Timothy's name scrawled on the bottom. Shaky writing, as if signed in a hurry. Or on horseback.

"That's all I want to know," Walt said grimly.

"That damned nester!" swore Maitland. "Walt, you should have run him off long ago."

Ben Anthony stopped Walt as the old man started for his horse.

"Here, hold your wolf awhile," he pleaded. "Calm down. I've known Tim Melvin a long time. So have you men. Nobody ever accused him of stealing before."

"He has killed our stock for beef," Rex thrust in.

"So what?" countered Ben. "That's done every day in this country. I recall Walt there telling Melvin to help himself to a yearling whenever his folks needed meat. No harm in that."

"So I did," growled Walt. "And this is the way he pays me back."

Across the street Harry Odell had been watching from the saloon. Now he came out, and called to them.

"You men come across for a drink."

He was grinning to himself. His ruse had worked. He could tell by Walt's red face how angry was his future father-in-law. And that Earnest temper was a terrible thing.

"Haven't time," Walt said curtly.

Odell sauntered closer, indolent, careless. The man was the picture of innocence.

"What's the trouble?"

"Tim Melvin raided Walt's stock," Keith Maitland volunteered.

Harry showed faint, fleeting surprise, then shrugged his shoulders. "Well," he said carelessly, "nesters eat somehow. They don't raise stock of their own, and they don't make enough farming to keep a gopher alive. Can't say I'm surprised."

Walt regarded his future son-in-law with accusing eyes. "You've been working close to those flats, you and your crew," he barked. "See any signs of Melvin rustling?"

"No-o-o," was Harry's slow answer, as if taken back by this sudden inquiry. Then, as if recollection was just breaking across his face; "I did see Tim skulking around that old line cabin of yours, halfway up the canyon. I was across the gulch, but he was slaughtering something. It might 'a' been a deer, of course. Tim hunts a lot."

He was clever enough to add this lame explanation. Walt whirled on Keith and Rex.

"Let's ride out and look around that cabin," he proposed.

The two Maitlands readily agreed.

"Mind if I ride with you gents?" Ben Anthony asked.

"Yes," snapped Walt. "If we find anything, we're riding on to settle with Tim. Right now. You're a town man. Stay out of it."

"I just want to point out," Ben said slowly, "that Tim hasn't done much rustling of his own. Did one man drive off the stock you missed last night?"

"No," Walt conceded. "But any kind of rustling calls for action. I don't mind Melvin killing a yearling for beef, but this slaughtering for hides and tallow plumb riles me. If Tim has killed a steer of mine for that purpose, I'll pull on him."

"Hear Tim's side of the story," appealed Anthony. "He's lived around here a long time without turning crook."

"Are you taking up for Melvin?" Walt Earnest hadn't lost his quick blazing temper in these sixty-four years.

"Mebbe," Ben said curtly. He had his temper, too.

Harry Odell watched them with confident amusement. Ben's defense of Timothy Melvin, Ben's insistence that they act lei-

54

surely, was only spurring Walt Earnest on to driving action. Walt was that stubborn, and Ben should have known it. He might have stopped them from riding right out to Tim's by pretending to be even more eager for an immediate showdown.

Walt glared at Ben a moment, then wheeled off to his horse. The Maitlands followed him.

Ben shook his head. "I sure hate to see Walt going off half-cocked," he sighed to Harry.

"Better sit out this hand," said Harry with some nervousness. The idea suddenly occurred to him that Ben Anthony might try to stop this. He knew his friend's capacity for always taking the side of the underdog, and seeing it through.

"Sure enough, Ben," he urged, catching the big man's shoulder as Anthony started after Walt. "Take my word for it, Tim Melvin has been sniping at Walt's steers. I've known it a couple of weeks, but didn't want to start hell a-popping."

Ben fingered the bill of sale he held in his hand, the bill of sale forged by Harry Odell himself. "I guess so," he muttered, in reluctant concession. "I guess Tim was getting hard up for cash. Why didn't the stubborn old fool come to see me?"

5

WALT and the two Maitlands rode in silence. It occurred to none
of them that it was strange for them to be riding together. In the
anger and the trouble of these times they had forgotten the feud
that had blazed between them, and that would blaze again when
the cattle world teetered back upright and there were rival outfits fighting for the free grass of the Chin-chin basin.

The Maitland brothers followed Walt up the rocky ledge into
the line cabin. There, just inside the door, where Caddo Parker
had carelessly tossed them, were the incriminating hides.

"The ————!" blazed Walt. His white mustaches quivered,
and his eyes were suddenly blood-red. "———— him! This is the
reward I get for letting a skulking nester live on my range."

"None of 'em ever spent a night on my place," Keith Maitland said grimly, "and none of them ever will."

"This is Tim Melvin's last," snapped Walt. He rolled into his
saddle, unsteady from his own boiling anger.

Keith and Rex Maitland followed close behind as he turned
off the main trail and into the clearing where Tim Melvin's small
house stood in the shade of spring-water elms. Melvin was cutting cedar posts a hundred yards away from the cabin; he heard
them coming and shouted a loud "Howdy," throwing his ax to
the ground and hurrying to meet them.

"Walt, dang it!" exploded this innocent nester. "You ain't
got any business gallivanting over the country like this. You
ain't a button any more."

Though one was a nester and one was the section's biggest
ranchman, they had been on friendly terms. Until today. More
than once Walt had stopped in this clearing for coffee, and he
and Timothy had talked man to man in the shade. They had

played checkers together on the small front porch in the cool of evening. A queer sort of pride had kept Timothy from ever returning these visits, but he had always welcomed the ranchman with quick warm hospitality.

He saw Walt's black anger and was shocked. "What's up?" he asked quietly, shooting his glance from Walt's beet-red face to the grim dark countenances of Keith and Rex Maitland, and back again.

Walt dismounted, breathing heavily from his fury and the exertion of his riding. He had been in the saddle most of the day.

"You got until daylight to get out," Walt Earnest said curtly. "If you're on my range by morning I'll shoot you down like a dog."

Timothy Melvin staggered from this verbal blow, like a badly wounded man, or a drunken one. Before the nester could answer, Agatha Melvin came out of the small cottage.

"Howdy, Walt Earnest," she called out. "I just put the coffee on. Stay a spell."

It was to her that Timothy spoke first. He turned to his wife, and she saw his troubled face and twisted her hands in her apron, knowing that it was no small thing which made him look so.

"No, Maw," the nester said in a quivering voice. "Walt has told us to be out by daybreak."

"Why, Walt Earnest!" exclaimed Agatha. "How can you talk so? After these long years!"

A wordless growl was Walt's only reply. Agatha plunged on, her voice now shrill with her own anger. "Have we ever bothered you and yours? Yes, we've taken some of your meat. But many a quarter of venison has my man packed down to your house, and many a mess of quail and fish. And I don't suppose you remember, Walt Earnest, who sat up day and night when your Minerva was dying? and who you came riding to when . . ."

Walt Earnest looked away from her. Damn a woman for always thrusting her nose in anyhow. This was no matter of personalities, but of thievery. The cheapest kind of thievery.

"You heard me, Tim," he growled. "It'll go hard for you if I ever see you on my range again."

Tim Melvin had turned toward his cabin; now, at Walt's repeated threat, at Walt's rude indifference to his wife, the nester wheeled back.

"Walt Earnest, I'll get off your land whenever you say the word," he snapped. "It belongs to you, and I'll never settle on a man's range without his say-so. You got the right to run me off, and I'm not going to make trouble. But don't take that threatening tone with me, man. I'm a human being, the same as you. I'll have you know that."

"No cattle thief is worth talking to like a man," exploded Walt. "Now start packing, damn you, before I bash your face in."

Timothy Melvin now was breathing as heavily as was the white-mustached ranchman.

"I don't take that kind of talk, Walt," he warned his old friend. "Ride off now before there is trouble. I'll get out of here in due time."

Agatha Melvin stepped forward, squarely between them. "Here, here," she begged, her eyes wide with fright. "You boys stop this bickering. Timothy Melvin, you come on and—"

She caught his arm, but her husband jerked free. "Lemme alone, Maw," Timothy said grimly. "Walt seems to have a notion all of a sudden that he can run over me."

"I want you off my range," Walt repeated.

"I told you I'd get off," Melvin shot back. "But I told you also to stop talking to me like I was a range rat. I won't be driven off like a slinking coyote, Walt Earnest. And if it's trouble you just got to have, we'll have it."

"Tim Melvin!" screamed Agatha.

A curse was Walt's first answer. Then he stood glaring down at the smaller, stouter nester a moment.

"So you're talking back!" he snarled. "I ain't forgot how to handle squatters, Melvin."

He rolled into his saddle, pitching a little. He took his lariat from the saddle horn and unwound it slowly.

"What are you going to do, Walt Earnest?" screamed Agatha.

"I'm gonna pull that shack down," vowed the Wide S owner. "I'm gonna set fire to it and—"

"Walt, you damned fool!" roared Melvin. "This is your land

but that's my shack. My things are in it. Touch it with your rope and—"

Melvin dived inside as he saw that Walt Earnest meant to carry out his threat. The nester bobbed back out of the door, his buffalo gun in his hand. Now Walt had looped one of the eaves and was backing his horse away. The two-room shack was stoutly built and the animal had to strain against the strength of the timbers.

"Walt, damn you!" raged Tim.

He threw the buffalo gun to his shoulder. Perhaps he would have pulled the trigger, perhaps not. The chance didn't come his way. Keith Maitland jerked out his revolver and shot swiftly. The rifle's charge went roaring off into empty space, and then the gun dropped from Tim Melvin's grasp to the ground, while the squatter suddenly caught his chest with both hands and staggered backward.

Agatha Melvin moaned and ran to her fallen husband. She cradled his head in her arms and stared up at Walt Earnest, who had ceased to pull on his lariat.

"You beasts!" she sobbed. "You've killed him. You and your temper, Walt Earnest. I hope you die from it."

Walt was staring down at the dying Melvin as if he could not believe his own eyes. He turned loose the lariat. He looked at Keith Maitland, who was still holding his smoking gun.

"Had to do it, Walt," Keith said with sincere regret. "He had a bead on you and was mad enough to kill you."

Walt nodded. Suddenly he felt weak and hollow inside. He looked at Agatha and his lips moved, but no sound came forth. Without a word to the Maitlands, he whirled his horse around and galloped toward his own house, his head low, his white mustaches drooping.

Behind him Keith and Rex Maitland exchanged looks, then also rode toward their own ranch. Agatha Melvin did not hear them go. All she could hear was the faltering last few breaths of her husband.

Melba Melvin rode slowly into the Odell yard and dismounted. Her face was chalk-white, and her eyes showed that she had shed many tears. Timothy had been a harsh father. Perhaps his sternness had been responsible for his daughter's easy yielding to Harry. Timothy had tried to teach with thunderous warnings instead of with gently spoken, reasonable explanations.

But he had been her father. And he was dead. Furthermore, her mother was moaning helplessly in the shack, and it was upon Melba's shoulders that the burden of caring for them fell. There was no one to turn to but Harry Odell. There was Tommy in town, but town was a long way.

Harry saw her coming and stalked over from the corrals, his face showing his determination to get rid of her. Already he had been advised of what had happened. It was not what he had expected. He had not foreseen Timothy Melvin's defiance of Walt Earnest's ugly humor, and the quick shot thrown by Keith Maitland to prevent Walt from being dropped by a blast of the buffalo gun.

Nor was this result what Harry had wished. Melba and her mother were still in this country. He had wanted Timothy Melvin to take them away. But now, at least, he did not have Timothy's buffalo gun to fear. And he could look down at Melba Melvin, white-faced and tearful though she was, and feel no pity.

She was too grief-stricken to notice then. "Harry!" she sobbed out, and ran into his arms before he could push her off.

For a moment he let her cry there. Then he snapped: "What's the trouble?"

As if he didn't know. It wasn't what he meant to say at all. It was only a preliminary to what he did intend to say.

"Walt Earnest and the Maitlands," the girl blurted, her whole body shaking. "They killed Pappy. They shot him down right in our front yard. Maw and me have got to pack up and leave, Harry. Walt Earnest will do something terrible if we try to stay there."

"Then you'd better get out of the country," Harry said coldly. "You know how ranchmen feel about nesters on their range. It's a wonder to me you could have stayed here so long."

Her head shot up in surprise and shock. Her dark troubled eyes searched his face.

"You didn't mean it!" she gasped. "You didn't mean what you told Pappy—about marrying me. You only told him that because he had his gun pointed at you. You never intended to—"

60

"Of course not," Harry snapped. "Your Pappy had the drop on me, there was nothing else I could say."

Melba laughed hoarsely. "Now you don't mind telling the world you were just fooling with me. Isn't that right, Harry Odell?"

"Just about," he said with a cold grin. "I'll help you and your mother get out of this country, Melba. I'll pay your stage fare somewhere else and even give you a little to start on. But you've got to get out. I'm not taking your side against Walt Earnest."

"Sure you won't," she said bitterly. "You're going to marry Bess Earnest. She's a ranchman's daughter, not a nester's gal. I'll bet you don't play around with Bess Earnest before you marry her."

Harry's face darkened. "That's none of your business," he snapped.

"No," admitted Melba, her mood changing from stormy bitterness to low sullen grief. "It's none of my affair. Sorry I came bothering you, Harry Odell."

"Wait a minute," he said, catching her arm. "I'm ready to help you, Melba. I'll send a wagon over and two men to help you pack. I'll put up the money for Tim's burial."

"No," she shot back. "I reckon Pappy would rather lie where he is than have *your* money bury him."

"Don't be a fool," begged Harry. He must get this girl out of the country before she spread her story. "Here," and he pressed a roll of bills in her hands. He had already prepared himself for this, and he considered the sum he was giving her very generous. Enough to see her father put away and buy her mother and herself stage tickets to another town. "I'll send a wagon over first thing in the morning."

Melba clutched the money without thinking. Then, with a sob, she threw it to the ground.

"No!" she cried. "I don't want it. To hell with you, Harry Odell!"

She fairly threw herself into the saddle and dug spurs into her pony. Harry Odell watched her ride off, at first in alarm, then with a cold smile. Finally, with a shrug of his shoulders, he retrieved the roll of bills. If she wanted to be a damned fool, what did he care? It would just save him money and trouble.

The speed of the ride, and the coolness of the wind in her face, partially soothed Melba's bitterness, and enabled her to ponder upon her plight with some calmness. She felt utterly helpless. For in other years the Melvins had always turned to Walt Earnest for help, as Walt had come riding for Agatha Melvin whenever sickness struck his house. Now, of course, she could not appeal to that quarter. Harry Odell had offered money and the use of a wagon, but Melba had some pride left.

What made her think of Ben Anthony, she did not know. Certainly Ben had never been more than a casual acquaintance of Tim Melvin, and always shy and aloof with her. As a boy he had sometimes hunted with her father—she could recall Timothy conceding that Ben was a top hand after a deer. Once Ben had ridden into Alice in the dead of night to bring a doctor for Melba's mother. But these were only casual courtesies, quickly granted without obligation entailed, and Melba realized before she ever reached Alice's dusty street that she was presuming a lot.

But where else could she go?

She found Ben in his small office laboriously bringing his stagecoach records up to date. He greeted her gravely, and rather awkwardly. He knew what had happened at her father's clearing. News like that traveled swiftly.

"Howdy, Melba," he murmured.

"Howdy, Ben," she whispered. She looked at him, and then off. She couldn't ask him for help, not for the life of her.

But she had come to a man who had a quick inborn sympathy for all kinds of men, and for women when his shyness did not keep him at arm's length.

He sighed and pushed his papers aside.

"I guess," he murmured, "we have lots of things to see about, Melba."

She nodded, still speechless.

Ben twirled his pencil around and around in his hand. "This is always sad business," he observed. "We've got to get Tim into town and buried. And I suppose you want to get off Walt's range as quick as you can?"

She nodded, still unable to speak.

"There are a couple of rooms downstairs at the hotel," he

62

mused. "Real private. That will do until we find something. Or you can decide what you want to do."

Another silent, tearful nod.

"I imagine Tommy is already out there," he said, referring to her brother. "I sent him out with a wagon as soon as I heard. Didn't you pass him on the way?"

Melba shook her head. She hadn't ridden back to the clearing from Odell's. Had instead cut across the ridge straight to town.

Ben stood up. "Let's ride out and see what's happening," he suggested.

Melba caught his arm. "I want to tell you something," she said. And, before she could stop herself, she had blurted out the story of her relations with Harry Odell.

Ben listened with tight lips. He was not too surprised. He knew that his friend was a man who was found attractive by women, and was attracted by them. He knew more about Harry's affairs with other valley girls than his friend would have guessed.

"Why are you telling me this?" he asked gently when she had finished.

"Mebbe, when you know that," she faltered, "you won't want to help us."

"I reckon women have made mistakes before," Ben said dryly.

He was immediately sympathetic with her, and yet also worried. He had his loyalty to Harry Odell to consider, and that loyalty was unaffected by this confession. He had known this about Harry before. Harry could no more resist women than he could deny himself the appeal of reckless living. That was Harry Odell, and a friend took a man for what he was. Then Ben Anthony had another loyalty, to Walt and Elizabeth Earnest. He must do what he could to soften the resentment valley people would feel for Timothy Melvin's killing when the first rush of anger had waned. Popularity with his neighbors meant something to the white-mustached old man.

Then there was Bess herself, whose happiness had been jeopardized by Harry Odell's recklessness. If this story got out over the valley, that Odell had seduced Melba Melvin, Bess would call off their wedding in a huff. And would never again consider Harry Odell as a prospective husband.

The thought never occurred to Ben Anthony that he held Harry's chances of marrying Bess Earnest in the palm of his hand. He was under no illusions as to his own feeling toward Walt's slim brown-haired daughter; he wanted her with a terrible aching of his whole frame, and he never tried to convince himself otherwise. But the idea of seeing that this story got to Bess Earnest, and taking his chances on the subsequent reward, did not enter his head.

Melba was still talking, her voice bitter. "He won't marry me, and I don't want him to," she sobbed. "It was Pappy's idea. I don't want to see him again."

"Do you want to leave the country?" Ben asked hopefully.

That would be the easy way. There was a stage leaving for San Antonio in the morning. They could rush Timothy's burial and get the Melvins' personal belongings back, and Tommy could carry their effects up later on the next freight wagon.

"I have some pull in San Antone," he added modestly. That he did. There was a restaurant there built to accommodate stage passengers. And it was doing well. The accompanying hotel was not Ben's property but he had loaned its owner money to set it up. "I think I could get you a job there. Mebbe your mother, too. I'd see you are taken care of if you go to San Antone."

Melba thought this over. Suddenly she felt no uneasiness before this big sympathetic man. Suddenly it seemed the most natural thing in the world that she was talking over her plight with Ben Anthony, and that he was advising her and offering security against the insecurity of tomorrow.

"Couldn't I stay here, Ben?" she asked after a moment. "This is the only country I ever knew. We've suffered some, but I don't like the idea of going somewhere else."

"Would you be happy here?" he asked. "Harry will always be around. Talk may start in spite of all we can do to keep it under our hats."

He did not say so, but he was afraid that Harry might launch such a rumor himself, in a boastful moment.

Melba did not answer. Ben continued, hoping to persuade her that she should leave.

"What could you do here?" he asked. "Work in the restaurant?

64

Work for me here? Marry? You'd have to do that, Melba. There is no place in this country for a woman who isn't married."

She nodded. "I know that." She sighed. "I wish I could hope that some man would want me, Ben. But I've had only one offer— of marriage. That was from Fritz Warner."

"Fritz!"

"Yes." Melba said with a short bitter laugh. "For a while he was always after me. Rode over almost every night. But he found out about Harry. He tried to warn me that Harry was just playing with me. I can see now that Fritz meant well. I told him" —her cheeks reddened—"that I'd rather be Harry Odell's plaything—than his wife."

Ben pursed his lips. "Naturally he didn't come back," added Melba. "I doubt if he will again."

"Do you want him to come back?" Ben questioned.

"I don't know," sighed Melba. "I like him some. He works hard. He is honest. I think he is a good man. It was only when I compared him to Harry Odell—as I saw Harry then—that I couldn't stand him. Mebbe now, feeling about Harry like I do, never wanting to see him again, I could look at Fritz in a different way. If he gave me the chance."

Ben Anthony hesitated. She did not want to leave the Jim Wells country. She was not afraid of staying here, and of perhaps facing the talk of the neighborhood which would inevitably find out. Many secrets were kept in this raw new land, but not this kind. It was a broad and free country—for a man. It was narrow and old for a woman.

"Well, let's ride out to your clearing," he proposed. "We'll get Tim's body into town and see about a funeral. Then, after a couple of days, we'll see what's what."

Melba nodded. She rode with Ben back over the trail to the clearing where she had lived all of her life. A mile from the cabin they sighted Ben's wagon, with Tommy Melvin in the front seat. The back was piled high with household possessions. On the shaky bed, set upright in the wagon, Agatha Melvin lay moaning.

Tommy pulled up the wagon and stepped out. Ben also dismounted.

65

Melba's brother was a slight serious-faced youth with clear gray eyes and set lines around his mouth. For a year now he had been Anthony's first assistant. Ben had the utmost confidence in him.

"I got everything," Tommy said. "I'll rig up a camp in the wagon yard if you don't mind."

"Take your mother and sister to the hotel," Ben vetoed. "They eat at the restaurant until they get settled. And go down to Morgan's and tell him I'm standing good for the expense."

"No call for that," Tommy said slowly. "You've helped enough. We'll get by. It won't hurt Maw and Sis to camp out until I can throw up a cabin. If you'll sell me some of that land off the wagon yard, I can build a house close to work and—"

Ben caught Tommy's shoulder between his fingers and squeezed it. This was a nester family, but there was good blood in them. In all of them.

Tommy looked past his employer to his sister. "Maw told me about the spat Pappy had with Odell," he said quietly. "That's nobody's business but ours. Reckon we'll call that water under the bridge."

Melba opened her mouth as if to explain that she had already confessed to Ben Anthony. Ben quieted her with a warning look.

"You go on to the hotel," Ben told Tommy as he remounted. He looked down from the saddle with a grin. "You ain't running this spread yet, young fellow. We'll talk about that house after the funeral."

He tipped his hat to Melba and rode off, spurring the big bay to a quick gallop.

Tommy Melvin looked after him with moistening eyes. "Ain't he sumpin'?" murmured the youth.

"Yes," Melba agreed, a catch in her throat.

"See what you can do about cheering Maw up," Tommy said briskly, aware of his new responsibilities again. "I'll tie your horse behind the wagon."

6

Ben found Fritz Warner branding yearlings in a stout corral built of cedar and mesquite posts.

At first the Chin-chin valley had snickered at this quiet solid Dutchman who was fool enough to think he could buy a section of land and make a go of cattle raising. But now Fritz had added another section, and other Jim Wells cattlemen were conceding that he was a worker and a good man with yearlings.

The German was willing to do what no other ranchman would accept as necessary—work with his own hands from before sunup until after dark, raising the necessities of life in addition to cattle. His herd did not have free run of even these two sections; but he flooded a small flat from a small irregular spring, to encourage his grass. He had a garden, which he irrigated, and he put up with his own hands jars of preserves and cans of vegetables. Then he had chickens and even a milch cow.

Fritz Warner seldom had many cattle to sell. But he had little need for cash. All his wants were met here, and he was gradually building up the balance of his credit at Marvin Sledge's bank.

There were claims that the German sometimes rode away from his own sections and searched other men's ranges until he found unbranded calves, which he drove back to his cedar-fenced range. Otherwise, it was argued, how could he build up his stock so quickly?

Marvin Sledge, who handled his account, could have defended the German if he had been so inclined. Fritz had never sold off anything but a cull, and his herd had built itself up faster than his neighbors' because he seldom lost a calf to coyotes or disease.

And his spread, surrounded as it was by cedar-post fences, was entirely too inaccessible for outlaws like Caddo Parker to bother with. He lived on his garden and his chickens.

Ben Anthony worked with Fritz until they had branded the last yearling. As they worked, they talked of casual things: the weather; the price of cattle. Fritz asked about Sledge's tallow vats, which he had never seen, and Ben described them.

The last calf branded, Fritz invited him to the house and brought out a pitcher of buttermilk cooled in the shade. Ben accepted a glass with a chuckle. It wasn't this country's usual choice of liquid, but he approved.

Finally he mentioned the nester's death.

Fritz nodded. He had heard of it. "I'm sorry," he said slowly. "I liked Timothy Melvin. He was a good man."

"That leaves Melba without a roof," Ben added. "A fine girl. She'll make some man a good wife."

Another nod from the stolid German. But no change of expression.

"I talked to her awhile ago," Ben murmured. He didn't relish this job he had taken on himself. He didn't play the role of John Alden very well. "She's changed. I guess a death does that to a young un. Makes 'em grown up and solid all at once where they were flighty and quick on the trigger before."

Fritz lit his pipe and puffed on it silently.

"She kinda let her hair down talking to me," Ben mused. "I dunno why, unless she figgers I'm a sympathetic soul. She told me about your sparking her, Fritz. Funny thing, she likes you."

Fritz grunted.

"Yeah, I know, there was Harry Odell," shrugged Ben. "He's the type of man who has a woman clawing for air the minute they set eyes on him. Me and you, Fritz, we ain't lady killers. I guess we gotta concede a guy like Harry an edge in that department, and go along and do the best we can."

There was more than sympathy for Fritz Warner in Ben's voice. He was comforting himself as well.

Another grunt.

"That business with Odell is all over," Ben said. "I guess there ain't a girl in this valley who ain't been crazy about Odell at one time or another. I wouldn't worry about it too much if I were you, Fritz. Odell, I mean."

"I do not worry about Odell," Fritz said crisply. "But Melba, she told me—"

"I tell you, she's changed. She'll be staying at my hotel in town for a few days. Drop in and see her, Fritz. Find out for yourself whether or not I'm talking through my hat."

"That I will do," Fritz promised.

Ben Anthony stood up. "Enjoyed the work. And the milk. I'll buy you a drink next time you're in town, Fritz."

The German nodded. When Ben looked back from a quarter of a mile off, he was still standing in front of his house, motionless as a statue.

Ben chuckled to himself. "I'll bet he's in town within forty-eight hours," he murmured.

The wagon bearing the Melvin possessions was still on the trail when he reached Alice. He had timed himself to beat Tommy to Morgan Mann's. Morgan carried the only ready-make caskets in this country.

"Hear about Timothy?" Ben asked.

The storekeeper clucked sympathetically. "Too bad," he said. "We needed more Timothy Melvins. I'm sorry old Walt lost his temper."

"He'll hate it worse than we do," Ben predicted, knowing the fits of remorse that followed the old ranchman's displays of temper. "What I wanted to see about, Morgan, was a casket for Timothy. Tommy is coming in here after a while. He's a stiff-necked little devil, and he may try to pay you out of what he has saved up. Try not to take his cash. If he's just hell-bent on paying you, put the price down dirt-cheap. I'll stand good for the difference."

Morgan regarded his knuckles thoughtfully. "That's the second time somebody has tried to pay me for Tim's casket," he said slowly.

"Yeah? Who else?"

"Walt Earnest."

"I might have guessed that," Anthony nodded. "Well, I can afford it better than Walt. Let Tommy have the casket down cheap, Morgan. He doesn't know anything about what caskets cost."

Morgan chuckled. "What are you trying to do, Ben—play Santa Claus to the whole damned country?"

"What do you mean?"

"How many broke waddies are you feeding? You're staking two ranches that I've heard about—Odell's and the Wide S. Now you're taking over the Melvins. I guess they're moving into your hotel and eating at your restaurant?"

"For a few days," Ben admitted.

"Next thing," Morgan grinned, "you'll be going after Caddo Parker's gang singlehanded."

"No," Ben declined. "My cash comes cheap, I'll lend it the same way. But not my hide. Fighting Parker isn't my business."

"I wish it was," sighed Morgan. "Ben, this whole danged country is going straight to hell unless somebody stops this dirty work. I'm flat again. You might as well cancel that load I ordered from Isabel."

Ben frowned, and cast a speculative look around Morgan's shelves. "You need it," he said. "You're not carrying stock enough now."

"I've let it out on credit," wailed the storekeeper. "I'm like you, Ben. I can't turn anybody down. This I got will go out the same way. Then I'll lock the door and bum you for a job."

Ben nodded. He could understand Morgan's plight. How could a storekeeper refuse credit to men like Keith and Rex Maitland, Alan Cameron, Walt Earnest, Harry Odell?

"I've done all I can," Morgan went on, his voice trembling. "Two years ago I was a rich man. I've got thirty thousand dollars due me, Ben. I guess I bit off more than I could chew. I wanted the trade of those outfits in Duval and along the Falfurrias slopes, and I went after it. There ain't a way out for me, Ben. I might as well close up today."

"I'd hate to see you close, Morgan," Ben said slowly.

Morgan shot Anthony a quick studying glance. "You're the only man that can save my store, Ben."

"I got some money," Anthony admitted. "You can have a loan. Just name it."

"I don't want a loan from you," Morgan shrugged. "I don't

70

want to keep in business that way. But I've been thinking, Ben. What are you doing with your profit? Are you going to buy more stages and open another freight line?"

"I don't think so," Ben said. "I like staying here, Morgan. I can't operate much further away than San Antone or Brownsville. Besides, I'd run into competition there. I guess I'll hang on to what I got, and try to pile up a little cash."

"There are two ways to get rich," Mann mused. "There is playing a market short, playing it to drop. There is playing it to go up. I learned that up East, Ben. Men up there buy and sell shares, guessing which way the wind will blow. Sledge, now, is playing this panic to stay. He's got things going his way. He is foreclosing right and left in Duval County, bringing their herds here, slaughtering 'em for hides and tallow. I ain't saying that Sledge is working with Caddo Parker right here in our valley. But I ain't seen signs of Caddo having any tallow vats. Yet he ain't leaving carcasses strewn around."

"No," Ben admitted. "He isn't."

"Sledge is coining dough. I saw my chance a year back. But it ain't my nature to play a country to go down, Ben. Seems to me that's what a buzzard does, hang around and wait for something to die. I'm playing this cattle country to come back—and men like Walt Earnest and Keith Maitland to stay. It looks like I went broke doing it, but that's the only way I'd draw to a hand."

"Me, too," Ben said. He recalled the chance Sledge had given him, to buy up ranch paper at a discount and then to foreclose.

"It's gotta last awhile," Morgan said gloomily. "There won't be a yearling sold in the next sixty days except for skinning. If every man sold his herds for hides and tallow, it'd be only a drop in the bucket compared to the paper Sledge holds against their grass. He's got this country on a downhill pull, Ben. But, my friend, *but*. If a man like me could hang on another year, could keep these outfits eating, could keep their credit business, until cattle prices come back, he'd be rich. Filthy rich, Ben. Sledge is working on a 6 per cent profit. I'm working on a 20 per cent margin."

"I see," nodded Ben. What was Morgan Mann telling him all of this for? What did Morgan have in his mind?

"Now is the time for me to expand," Morgan said. "Stores are down at Falfurrias and George West. I could push my trade for a hundred miles in any direction. All of these ranchmen will pay up when they get money. And they ain't the type of men to forget who carried 'em through. I've got ideas, Ben. I've been thinking of expanding into a big outfit. Selling saddles and staples by mail. Delivering 'em."

Ben's eyes gleamed. Freighting was his business. "Now you're talking my language," he said.

"I hope so, Ben," Morgan Mann said quietly. "Because I got to have more than your wagons. I got to have your money."

"You can borrow it," Ben said again.

"No," Morgan snapped. "I want you as a partner."

Anthony hesitated. "That's throwing it at me kinda sudden," he hedged.

"Think it over," Morgan said. "I believe in this country, Ben. So do you. We'll play freeze-out with guys like Sledge who are trying to sell us out to the wolves. The firm of Mann & Anthony will stand behind the bigger outfits. We'll advance what cash we can. We'll shoot 'em staples and saddles and horseshoes right up to their gate. They ain't got the hands to do their own smithwork any more. You got a good shop. You got the wagons already. Some of the things don't even have to come to Alice. You can deliver 'em direct out of Port Isabel or San Antone."

"That's true," Ben conceded. His eyes were gleaming with approval of Morgan Mann's dream.

He pushed his hat back on his shoulders. "I think you got a partner, Morgan," he grinned.

"We can make it go. You're a shrewd trader, Ben. By paying cash in advance of delivery, you can run the prices down in Port Isabel and San Antone. We can operate on a 20 per cent mark-up and still sell cheaper than anybody in two hundred miles."

"I'll drop back later," Ben said. "It sounds good to me."

He went from Morgan's to the small hotel. Agatha Melvin had recovered from her grief, and greeted Ben calmly.

"Tommy has told me what you intend to do for us. You're a kind man, Ben Anthony. But none of the Melvins want charity. I've been through your kitchen. It's filty dirty. Those Mexican cooks don't know the first principles of turning out good food. I'm taking over this kitchen."

Ben started to protest; Agatha Melvin raised her hand.

"Don't argue with me, young fellow. You need help. You're too young a boy to get along without a mother's bossing. Do you want people riding through Alice on your stage to talk about how dirty your hotel is?"

"No," Ben shrugged.

Melba came in, mop in hand, a cloth tied over her hair.

"I've finished the upstairs rooms, Maw. What next?"

"We got to take this kitchen apart," sniffed Agatha. "There never was a man fit to clean up a kitchen, much less a Mexican."

Ben grinned and walked over to the wagon yard. The stage came clattering in, and a handful of passengers made for the restaurant. The driver paid a quick visit to the saloon. In a quarter-hour the freshly painted Concord coach was on its way again, weaving and bobbing down the dusty road. Tommy Melvin handed Ben a pile of invoices. Two loads of tallow to Port Isabel. A load of general merchandise for San Antonio.

A tall bearded man rode up as he was checking the invoices and asked for Ben Anthony.

"That's me," Ben admitted.

"My name is King," said the bearded man. "I run the Santa Gertrudis."

Ben nodded. He knew of this King, and the Santa Gertrudis. King and his partner owned a stretch of land that dwarfed all of the Chin-chin range. It spread from a half-day's ride from Alice to the Gulf.

"What's on your mind?"

"I want to contract for delivering hay to my ranch," explained King. "Have you got the wagons to handle it?"

"Oh, I guess," Ben said carelessly. He was thinking of a wagon-load or two. Most ranchmen were not feeding hay to their steers, only to their remudas. "How many you want?"

"If you can handle it," snapped Captain Richard King, "I want a thousand loads per mouth until spring."

"That," murmured Ben, "is a heap of hay."

Captain King did not answer.

"But I guess," Ben added in the same slow speech, "you got a heap of land. And cattle." He rolled a cigarette. "Been wanting to meet you, Captain King, let's wet our whistles over at the saloon."

"Look, friend," King said impatiently. "If you can't handle the contract, say so. I didn't ride over here just to have a drink."

"I'm figgering on making you another proposition," Ben drawled. "Buying supplies for a ranch like yours must be a man-size job. I guess you have all kinds of trouble getting 'em shipped in."

"I send my wagons to Port Isabel," snapped King. "I buy my own."

"What if I put supplies for your ranch right at your front gate?" Ben asked. "Staples. Horseshoes. Iron. Saddles. Leather. You make a list of what you want, I get it there."

"I'm afraid we can't make any such agreement," King said briskly. He didn't have the lazy drawl of most Texans. "At Port Isabel I have arrangements with a bank to advance me whatever I need. From season to season. I don't carry enough cash around with me to meet due bills."

"A man's a fool to," Ben nodded. "Reckon your credit's good with me, Captain King."

Richard King stared at this huge young man who talked so carelessly of supplying his huge ranch with a season's commodities on credit.

"Are you bluffing," he demanded, "or are you ignorant of the Santa Gertrudis' size?"

"Reckon I know about the size of your spread," Ben said mildly. "Close to a million and a half acres, ain't it?"

"Almost," Richard King smiled. "And you have the cash to carry my ranch from season to season?"

"I guess."

Ben rolled a cigarette. "In fact, I was thinking the other day about toting your hides and tallow for you. Reckon I could keep a string of wagons busy at your place alone. You wouldn't have to buy your staples here. With a place your size I could bring 'em straight from Port Isabel. My podner and me have been thinking about opening a clearinghouse there anyhow."

"I'll take the drink," Captain King agreed. "I like the way you talk, young man. And let me tell you, you're starting in a fine business. I was a freighter before I ever bought an acre of land."

Ben nodded. He knew that. King and his partner, Kennedy, had operated steamboats along the Gulf coast.

Morgan Mann was sent for, and chuckled as Ben outlined his proposal.

"Of course," Ben said to Captain King, "Morgan here has to agree. We're partners."

"Do you think you can handle it?" King demanded of the storekeeper.

"It's a deal," Morgan said promptly.

Captain King bought a round. He regarded Ben Anthony with a thin smile.

"Have you guessed at the profit you'll make annually off the Santa Gertrudis ranch?" he demanded.

"Well, I made a swift calculation," Ben admitted.

"I'd say forty thousand a year," King predicted. He motioned to the barkeeper. "A young man not thirty years old who can close a deal like that in a half-hour should buy another round," he said curtly.

But the Santa Gertrudis owner did not tarry long. Morgan looked after him with a sigh.

"It scares me, Ben," he said. "You're the dangedest guy. I just mention something to you, and before you've even told me for certain you're in with me you've sewed up a contract like this."

"He just rode in," shrugged Ben. He studied the rim of his glass. "I'll be in Port Isabel a few days. We have to set up a warehouse there, Morgan. And start buying in bigger lots. In whole boatloads."

"I've been thinking the same thing," said the storekeeper. "You go on to Isabel and set up the warehouse. I'll take the stage for Galveston and talk to a guy who owns some steamers. Then I'll take a boat to New Orleans. I can get a pretty good discount by buying a year's stock in advance."

"How much will it take as a deposit?"

"I think nothing," Morgan said. "I got a good credit rating. If I have to put up cash, can I draw a draft on you here?"

"Either here or at the Cattlemen's National in San Antonio," Ben answered. "Keep most of my cash there. But Sledge has enough to handle a fair-sized draft."

Ben returned from Port Isabel to find his hotel and restaurant completely rejuvenated—fresh paint, gleaming counters, polished floors, and fresh vegetables on the menu in addition to the proverbial steak and potatoes. Behind the counter was Melba Melvin.

"Howdy, stranger?" she smiled.

"Your maw," Ben murmured, "seems to have been working."

"Do you like it?"

"Muy bueno."

"She always has wanted to feed people," Melba laughed. "I guess you're stuck with her."

"You brighten up the place yourself," Ben said. "Are you going to be a regular ornament?"

"Well," she said slowly, looking off, "I don't think so."

"What's going on?"

"Fritz has been in a lot," Melba answered, a spot of crimson showing in each cheek. "He still wants me, Ben."

"Fritz is a good man. You could do worse, Melba."

"I guess," she sighed. "I'm not sure. But . . . Oh, I am sure, Ben! There's nothing else for me to do."

"Fritz," repeated Ben, "is a good man."

"Worth a handful of Harry Odells," Melba said bitterly. "I guess we'll get married right away. Fritz is in a hurry, and I've no reason for putting it off."

"I'll throw the wedding," Ben promised.

7

BEN found Harry Odell in the comfortable house, at his ease with a drink in his hand. It was still midafternoon, and Ben wondered how a man who owned such a ranch could stay off its trail in this kind of weather. He wanted to reprove Harry, but held his tongue.

What Ben felt for this good-looking, seemingly indifferent man was hard to explain. Certainly it was not the admiration of one strong man for another, not a friendship founded upon mutual respect. Things had always come easy to Harry Odell, dirt-hard to Ben Anthony. The superior faculties Anthony possessed had been developed by grim necessity.

Perhaps his feeling for this close friend was a desire to protect Odell from what he had never been exposed to, and wouldn't know how to cope with if it came along.

"Sit down for a drink," the ranchman said cordially. "I'm gonna ride over to Walt's for supper. Come along."

"I was thinking of doing that. Haven't paid the Wide S a visit in quite a spell."

Harry brought whisky, and Ben tossed a glass down. His host also drank another.

Ben eyed the half-empty bottle. "Drinking much, podner?" he asked.

"Always trying to reform me," grinned Harry. "No, you big ox, I'm doing all right."

"Good!" Ben accepted a cigar, lit its tip, and regarded its amber glow thoughtfully. "I just talked to Melba Melvin in town. She is gonna marry Fritz Warner."

Harry started. He had viewed the Melvins' presence in town with alarm. He had even fumed that Ben was giving them sanctuary. But this was a welcome solution to his problem. Now there would be no talk.

"Thank God!" he sighed.

He regretted that his relief told his friend the whole sordid story if he did not know it already.

"You nearly got in trouble there, podner," the big man said quietly. "You're getting hitched in the spring. Can't you leave these valley girls alone that long?"

"I sure can," was the hearty response. So happy was Harry Odell to be rid of Melba that he didn't even resent such advice from the big man.

Ben wanted to say more. He wanted to point out that Harry should sometimes consider the results left in the wake of his intense concentration upon satisfying his own demands. But it was hard for a friend to talk so bluntly. And Ben Anthony was essentially a man of action, not words.

"What's this I hear about you and Morgan going partners?" Harry asked.

"Yes."

"And you've landed a contract with Richard King? Before long, Ben, you'll be filthy rich."

"If this panic breaks by winter," shrugged Ben, "we'll be doing all right. How are things out here? And at Walt's?"

"Fair, I guess," was the careless answer.

In the past few days Caddo Parker and his gang had been concentrating operations in Duval County, raiding outfits who were holding up against Sledge's foreclosure threats. Harry's own vaqueros were still working the brushy flats for unbranded cattle, and the Dollar Mark again had more steers than it could feed. Harry would have to trail another three hundred head at least over to Sledge's. But he told his friend only part of this:

"I'm selling some more to Parker. No use of keeping anything but yearlings and stockers."

"No," agreed Ben, "there isn't. You got a full range, Harry; I noticed that as I rode through. Kinda funny the Maitlands and the Camerons are getting so thin."

Harry shot the big man a quick glance. Was he voicing suspicion? "Let's ride on over to Walt's," he proposed.

Ben was ready. They loped around the shoulder of the ridge,

following a trail they had ridden as boys. Harry was suddenly in a very gay mood. He recalled the time he had been fighting all three of the Cameron boys when Ben rode over the hill to his rescue, and had licked two of the Camerons singlehanded.

"They never bothered me again," Harry said with a chuckle.

They came out of the hills upon the Wide S headquarters from the back, and Ben's lips twitched. He never saw Walt Earnest's corrals and house without feeling homesick. Perhaps Walt, or the fate he represented, had been more cruel to Ben Anthony than kind. It was heartbreaking to have a home and a range, and to love it; then, when old enough to understand such things, to realize of a sudden that it wasn't his at all, that he owned nothing about it but his memories.

Ben had met that heartache, but had never conquered it.

Walt Earnest, repentant and glum, gave them no more than a nod and stalked off to the corral with the muttered explanation that he had to see about his horse.

"I'm glad you came," Bess said. "This Melvin business has Dad broken up."

"Not the end of the world," Harry said lightly. "Timothy isn't the first nester to pay a price like that for sneaking onto a man's range."

"But it was so unnecessary," the girl sighed. "Besides, he wasn't bothering anybody."

"Just stealing stock."

"I'm not convinced of that," Elizabeth declared. "There were some Wide S hides in a line cabin. On that proof, and no more, Tim Melvin was shot."

"And Ben had a bill of sale signed by Timothy Melvin."

"Did you, Ben?"

Ben nodded.

"It's hard to believe," Elizabeth still insisted. "Tim was always so honest."

"They're being well taken care of," Harry pointed out. "The whole family is in now where Uncle Ben can look after 'em."

Bess cooked biscuits at Harry's plea. Ben, smiling thinly, watched his friend mold her with his fingers. Harry Odell certainly had a way with women.

Walt came back from the corral just before supper. He smoked his pipe silently, staring at the two young men in an absorbed study. Any effort to include him in their conversation was futile. He wolfed his meal and went off to bed with the first layers of darkness.

Harry and Ben helped Bess with the dishes. Then the three of them walked outside and to the well, where they perched on the stone rim and chatted casually of valley affairs.

Shortly Ben said it was time to go. He was always a little self-conscious when he was alone with the two. Harry Odell had never dropped an intimation, nor had Bess, but Ben felt that for them it was a case of two being company and three a crowd. At least, if Bess Earnest has been *his* fiancée and Harry Odell had been the third, for the ride, such would have been his feeling.

"Wait a minute and I'll ride into town with you," Harry proposed.

"Don't rush off," begged Bess. "I've been shut up here with Dad all week. He's hardly said a word since the shooting."

"I'll brighten you up a little," Harry chuckled, and reached for her.

"Don't, you idiot!" But Bess was not angry with him. No woman could be. She resisted him a moment and then surrendered her lips to his for a quick kiss.

His arms still around her, Harry grinned at his friend. "That's one thing I could teach you, Ben," he gloated. "You know how to make money where I go broke. You know how to use a gun and a rope, and you can ride any horse you ever saw. But do you know how to kiss a woman? I'm afraid not."

The vines growing around the well threw dark shadows over them that hid Ben Anthony's face. It was just as well. Yearning was written there, and envy. What he ached for, what he had dreamed about before lonely campfires and on wet dark trails, Harry Odell could take with a grin, could take with a light jesting force and yet leave no rancor. There was no point in Bess Earnest's pro-testing that she did not want to kiss Harry Odell; he would have kissed her anyhow. Harry had the gift of daring—with women. Ben had urges of recklessness and sometimes the genius of reck-lessness; but not with a woman, any woman—Bess Earnest least of all.

He forced himself to grin; he mustn't show his resentment of this taunting, and the trend of this teasing.

"I ain't ever been in competition with you, podner," he answered. As if he hadn't been in competition with Harry Odell, as much as he dared, all his life!

"You wouldn't stand a chance, Ben," Harry said confidently. "I guess I ought to take time off and give you lessons. You're too rich to be a bachelor."

Carrying the lightness of their mood even further, he pushed Bess into Ben's arms. "Here, you big ox. Try your hand, and see if you can come up to Odell's standard. I guess the only way I can prove to you that you aren't in my class is to show you up by comparison."

Elizabeth Earnest did not push back. She seemed to be caught in the wave of Harry's humor, as they had usually been throughout their lives.

"I think Harry needs to be taken down a notch, Ben," she laughed, slipping one arm around the big man's neck.

Ben held her a moment, his hands on her shoulders, unwilling to accept this kiss that was meant in fun, yet obviously not willing to refuse. Bess lifted her face, and of a sudden his arms tightened until she was strained against him and his mouth covered hers with all the determined force that was Ben Anthony in other ways, but had never been expressed in this way before.

Bess raised both hands to his face as if to push him back, and for a second she was stiff and unyielding. But there was no pushing Ben back. The strain went out of her with a sigh, and she melted against him, and for a long moment they stayed like that, molded into what seemed a single shape in the darkness.

Finally he let her go. He could have laughed off the tenseness that all three of them felt. This had been only in play, and a dozen things he might have said would have told Harry Odell and Bess Earnest that he was only playing, too, taking up his friend's challenge in the light spirit in which it was issued. But he said nothing, and neither Bess nor Harry could speak. They were shocked. Harry felt some anger and resentment, but did not want to voice it. Bess was shaking with startled confusion and strange unexpected emotion; she could not speak of that, of course. And Ben, who didn't have the laugh or the jest when it was needed, felt a be-damned-to-you defiance. They had pushed him into it.

A man like Ben Anthony could never laugh off what he felt. After a moment he said, "I'm sorry," and that was not an apology at all. That was an admission of what he had shown. That was confirmation of what he had felt.

Harry Odell had intended to tease his friend after this kiss was over; but there was nothing teasing about Harry's feelings. For a long time no other word was spoken. The whiteness of the girl's face, and the tenseness of her slim body, were plain to see and feel.

Then Ben said: "I'll be riding. Thanks for the supper."

It was an awkward exit. He knew it. But he was an awkward sort of man except where the physical side of life was concerned. He could ride a horse as if welded to the animal, but he was ever clumsy and self-conscious when tipping his hat. His way out of a corner was not a smiling explanation, or a glib changing of the subject. Harry evidently had forgotten about going with him, and Ben did not wait.

His spurs made a bell-like sound as he went to his horse. Both Bess and Harry watched him swing up into the saddle. The drifting shadows magnified his size. They saw him wheel the bay around without looking back; the first pace the horse struck was a mad gallop, and the echoes kept drifting back to them, freezing the words they might have spoken.

Harry sensed that his fiancée was disturbed; and in his own heart was a mute wonder, and an angry wonder. Another man might have challenged her then and there, and, in that sudden strange mood of hers, she would have been quick with her defiance. But Harry Odell had an inborn smoothness. He was a little late with his change of subject, but he got there.

"I wish somebody would throw another dance. I haven't kicked up my heels in a long time."

"Yes," Bess murmured absently.

Harry realized that she hadn't heard his words. She was staring off into the night, oblivious to his presence. He was there, and she knew it. But at the moment he was an impersonal companion. He was just someone left there when Ben Anthony had gone.

His eyes narrowed. No mater what turn a man's mind takes, he can always look in the past, the long past and the short past, and see justification for this new idea. Funny that he had never thought of Ben as a rival before! There had been John Cameron awhile, but he had possessed the strong advantage of Walt's enmity to a Cameron, or to any man who ranched across the creek and fought with him for the grass of the flats. There had been a young man from town, an ambitious young doctor. After six months he had moved to San Antone. All the time, except for three years, there had been Ben Anthony, doggedly silent, solicitous of the Wide S's welfare beyond what ordinary gratitude to Walt Earnest called for.

Harry Odell felt a sudden panic. He had his egotisms, but also his deep consciousness of his own faults. And Ben Anthony would never be a stronger man, or a truer character, than Harry thought him. That quality was unshakable in Odell. He *knew* Ben. He had never sold Ben short, as many others who looked upon this big amiable man with slight condescension had done.

So Ben Anthony wanted Elizabeth Earnest. Elizabeth had never known it before this night. Harry, with some gift of human analysis, sensed that. But now Elizabeth knew it, and she was disturbed by it. Which meant that she, in some way, must be stirred by Ben's grim appeal.

Harry Odell's lips parted in a thin smile. So he and Ben were rivals! He and good old Ben, the only close friend he ever had. He was gripped in panic and wonder no longer. It was a little surprising that he bore Ben no malice. It occurred to him that it was only natural that Ben Anthony, who had been raised here, should share his own ambition to marry a ranch and a girl in the same move. So it was he and Ben Anthony at the showdown! Harry was pleased at his own reactions. He was pleased to find that he did not particularly fear Ben. As he had said earlier in the night, Ben could teach him a lot of things. Ben, far more than Harry, was a man of gifts. But this slim girl staring out in the moonlight was not a horse to be broken, a calf to be tied, or a freight wagon to be pushed through mud and sand to Port Isabel in time to catch a steamer. She was a woman, and Harry Odell had studied the science of appealing to women. And of eliminating his rivals.

"I understand," he said, "that Melba Melvin is going to marry Fritz Warner."

Elizabeth gratefully seized upon the chance of making idle conversation. "I'm glad. Melba is a nice girl."

"I don't know," Harry grinned. "I understand Tim Melvin had his buffalo gun oiled."

"Harry!"

This quality was among his worst, and certainly the one he could least control. Now, in his own eyes, he had a justification. So Ben Anthony wanted Bess Earnest!

"Well, that's the rumor," he shrugged. "I don't know, of course. But Ben seems willing to take care of 'em."

"Ben! Ben Anthony!"

Bess Earnest could not reconcile this. Ben Anthony seducing a girl!

"He's paying for it," Harry went on. "He's got the whole family on his hands now."

Bess nodded. Appearances were in Harry's favor. He was not the first to comment in her presence upon Ben's open-handed generosity toward the Melvins, and to insinuate that it was because of Melba's dark-haired voluptuous charm. But . . . Elizabeth hesitated.

"I don't believe it," she said firmly. There was a note in her voice which indicated that she did not *intend* to believe it.

"Surprised me," Harry shrugged. "Ol' Ben used to be as shy as a prairie dog around women. I guess he picked up a few tricks riding up the trail."

Bess recalled the savage passion of the big man's kiss and touched her lips gently. "Yes," she murmured, "I suppose he did."

Harry was wise enough not to press this subject further. He chuckled to himself as he rode across the ridge trail to his own Dollar Mark. What a night this had been! Well, he didn't doubt that he had thrown a halter around Ben Anthony's neck!

Behind him Bess Earnest prepared slowly for bed. From Walt's room finally came a snort.

"Are you going to gad about all night?"

"I don't seem to be sleepy, Dad," she apologized. Sleep was the last thing she wanted. It was strange how one moment a woman could be sure of herself, and the next instant be so confused.

For a moment there was no answer. Then she heard Walt's feet hitting the floor.

"Dang it, now you got me wide awake," he complained. "Brew us up some coffee."

8

Sᴌᴇᴅɢᴇ's first inkling of the partnership between Morgan Mann and Ben Anthony came when a draft for ten thousand dollars was delivered to him. It was payable to the Southland Produce Company in New Orleans. Anthony was in Port Isabel, and the banker could do nothing but fume until Ben returned. In the meantime, another draft arrived, drawn to the Gulf Coast Shipping Company.

This was not all that stirred the banker's curiosity. Tommy Melvin presented the first check from the Santa Gertrudis ranch for deposit. Sledge had modeled his own tallow vats after Captain Richard King's. He had sought King's banking business, only to be summarily rejected.

"Tell Ben I want to see him," Sledge told Tommy.

Ben obeyed the summons. Sledge fingered the two drafts. "You're getting in deep, Ben. Fifteen thousand is money even for you."

"I think it's a good deal," Ben said carelessly. "I've been aiming to pay you a visit anyhow. I want another account started, for the firm of Mann & Anthony. Morgan is entitled to check on it the same as me."

"You're partners with Morgan!" frowned Sledge. "That's risky, Ben. Morgan gives credit to every ranchman in this country."

"We're running that kind of business," Ben said shortly.

He knew how this partnership would set with Sledge. If cattlemen could get easy credit from Mann & Anthony, they wouldn't come to Sledge's bank for loans. And the banker was still loaning money where he had to. The Maitland, Cameron, and Earnest outfits were already in debt to him for enough to insure their foreclosure with another bad year. But Sledge was looking beyond this Chin-chin range, as were Mann & Anthony. Foreclosing was the simplest way of getting his hands on a herd. He was taking in cattle for a small percentage of their value. The hides went to Caddo, the tallow to Sledge. Not all of Parker's riding was beyond the law.

"I suppose," Sledge said slowly, drumming his fingers on the scarred top of his desk, "that there is no use advising you against this deal, Ben?"

"No," was the firm retort. "Morgan and me are gambling on the future of this country."

Sledge closed his eyes and made some swift mental notations. This scrawny little man knew almost to a penny how much it would take to carry this Chin-chin basin through another year. He doubted if Ben Anthony had that much, certainly not in his bank. But he couldn't take Anthony and Mann too lightly.

Harry Odell thought he was dealing in big stakes, but actually Harry was a piker compared to Sledge. The banker's lips tightened.

"Bueno," he murmured. "I'll honor the drafts. I hope you don't get your fingers burned, Ben."

"I'll give you a draft on the Cattlemen's National in San Antonio to take up the slack," Ben said, starting to write out the document.

Sledge started. So Ben Anthony had more cash there. With revenues pouring in from stage and freight lines, with the business of the King Ranch as a backlog, there was no telling how much financial punishment Anthony could take. Sledge knew that Richard King had enough wild cattle, in which he had practically no capital invested, to keep the Santa Gertrudis tallow vats running day and night, and the Santa Gertrudis operating on a ninety-day cash basis. For a brief time Sledge had even considered the possibility of clutching the King acres in his thin fingers. He had given that up as impossible. Richard King was too firmly established.

As soon as Anthony left, Marvin Sledge sent a messenger for Caddo Parker. He was more upset than he cared to admit. He had a respect for Anthony he didn't show for other men in this Chin-chin basin. Anthony had the understanding of a dollar, and the ability to juggle it.

Parker slipped in by a rear entrance and conferred with the banker in a small private room where he stored his securities.

"Parker," barked Sledge, "this Anthony is getting too big for his britches. Can we break him?"

Caddo Parker frowned. "What's wrong with Anthony?"

"He's got too much money," explained Sledge. "He has thrown in with Morgan Mann. They're going to carry ranchmen a full year. Clothes, shoes, equipment, and groceries. That'll play hell with our hides and tallow business."

"I dunno," shrugged Caddo. "We can still pick 'em up by night."

"Your boys average running off a hundred head per night," Sledge rasped. "That's chicken feed, Caddo. We can't depend on rustling alone."

"That's an ugly word, 'rustling,'" drawled Caddo. "Why not call it 'picking up strays'? If we get a branded cow or two by mistake, we're not to blame. Hard to see at night."

Sledge ignored the outlaw's attempt at levity. "Anthony is shipping in some valuable stuff. He's hauling tallow for Richard King. We could use what's in those wagons, Caddo."

"Could be," mused Caddo. "I know a fella in Corpus who would handle some hot cargo. But there ain't much profit, Sledge, I'll promise you that."

"But we'd be getting rid of Anthony," the banker pointed out. "Take his wagons, kill his drivers, burn his wagons, kill his mules."

"That is playing a mite rough," frowned Caddo.

"We've got to play rough," Sledge snapped.

"I need more boys," Caddo pointed out. "I don't want to risk the hands we pick up around the saloons for that. I want boys who can ride hard, shoot straight, and keep their mouths shut."

"So do I," agreed the banker. "Get 'em in here, Caddo."

"I need chips."

Sledge groaned. He never liked to part with a dollar. But he reached into his cash drawer and pulled out a thousand dollars in bank notes.

"This should be enough," he said gloomily.

"It'll do as a starter," grinned Caddo. "Boys like that need chips, Sledge. They drink a lot, and they got an eye for a pretty gal, especially a Mex. Got to keep 'em happy."

Caddo Parker left the bank grinning. In the first place, he liked to get Sledge over a barrel and make the tightwad cough up. In the second, he rather relished this coming feud with Ben Anthony. He walked with a swagger into the wagon yard. Ben had presented the dark-faced outlaw with a challenge that he yearned to take up. This Jim Wells country thought this Anthony was tough. Hell, they had never seen a tough guy in operation!

Ben and Tommy Melvin were working over two heavy wagons. Caddo watched in idle amusement. Ben picked up the rear of the wagon and held it singlehanded while Tommy removed a wheel. The guy was strong, Caddo was ready to concede that. But could he handle a six-gun? The Jim Wells country claimed he could. But what did this neck of the woods know about gunplay? Farther west, and up in the trail towns, Caddo had seen some fancy gun-slinging. He had done some himself.

As he watched, the Brownsville stage rolled in—a heavy serviceable Concord. The passengers made a rush for the near-by restaurant, where Melba Melvin was clanging a big cowbell. Caddo eyed the girl appraisingly. He wondered if she had taken up with Anthony, as saloon gossip sometimes hinted.

Among the passengers was Fritz Warner. The square-set German gave Melba a shy grin as he stood with her outside the restaurant.

"Look what I brought," he said triumphantly.

And he took a plush box out of his pocket and let her peep inside.

"Fritz!" exclaimed Melba, her face coloring.

"I must have such a ring," Fritz said awkwardly, wishing that he had the gallantry of a Harry Odell, "for such a wife."

Melba Melvin turned into the restaurant to hide her confusion. Fritz caught her shoulder. "Wait just a moment," he begged. "I have other things to tell you. I have new furniture coming from Brownsville. When it comes, and is in my house . . ."

She answered the unspoken question. "Yes, Fritz," she said softly. "We'll get married then."

She brooded over this promise as she helped her mother serve the hungry, thirsty passengers. Married to Fritz Warner! As soon as the stage had clattered on its way, disappearing into a cloud of dust, she hurried to her room and threw herself face down on her bed. She would go through with it. Fritz was her only chance. But she could only cry bitter tears as she viewed the future.

Anthony and Melvin finished repairing the wagon, and loaded it high with tallow from the King vats as the mule skinner came out of the saloon and regarded the completed job with the arrogance of his kind.

Ben Anthony's business had its complications. The wagon had broken down twelve miles from Alice and Ben himself had ridden to its rescue. Few drivers would stoop to the manual labor of repairing and loading wagons. That even some of Ben's Mexican helpers made more money than they did not bother the drivers: they had their dignity to fall back upon, they did not work with their hands.

But they were trustworthy. They were his representatives in Port Isabel and San Antonio, and they took their responsibilities seriously.

This driver had a short leg, lost because of a steer's horn in a Red River flood. He crammed his jaw full of tobacco and squinted at Ben.

"What's the layout, Ben?"

"Carry this tallow to King's agent at Port Isabel. Make him sign a receipt. Then pick up a load of merchandise at Hagan's."

Ben hesitated. He trusted Fuzz Knight's judgment about mules and wagons.

"You got drunk last night you were down there. Feel another coming on, or do you think you can stay sober?"

"I ain't recovered from the last one yet," grinned Fuzz.

"I need another wagon and another span of mules," Ben said. "Pete Crenshaw down there makes pretty good wagons. If he has one on hand, make a deal."

"Pete will skin you," warned Fuzz.

"Never has," said Ben. "This half-breed Vega usually has some pretty fair mules. But he's a crook from way back. Don't buy anything without studying 'em. Look at their teeth and eyes."

"Yeah," nodded Fuzz. "He dopes 'em sometimes. I'll take care of it, Ben. Vega won't sell me any half-live mule."

"Good," Ben said. He would trust Knight's judgment as quickly as his own. "Here's a thousand. Pay Vega cash for any mules you buy. Crenshaw will trust me for the rest if that doesn't cover everything."

Fuzz nodded. Credit was that easy in this country when a man was known. Anthony's drivers could buy on paper anywhere.

Caddo found Stubby Wright in Fatty's and, over a bottle, outlined his plans. Stubby listened avidly. He had ridden with Quantrell, and violence was to his liking.

"Do we split with Sledge?" demanded Stubby.

"We do *not*," snapped Caddo. "They've been outdealing me so far, him and this Odell. Now I've got Sledge where I want him. We'll clean up off this Anthony, Stub."

Wright nodded eagerly. He had been squirming under the small profits of hide and tallow rustling.

The two outlaws finished their bottle, then took the trail to Port Isabel. They circled around Fuzz Knight's wagon, toiling slowly and painfully along in the deep dusty ruts, and cooked their noon meal in the brushy flats below Robstown. Where the Pedernick River crossed the road, they set up their ambush.

Several hours later the wagon lumbered in sight. Caddo and Stub had been amusing themselves playing poker with a worn deck of cards. Caddo thrust the pack into his saddlebag and took his Winchester from its holster.

"Gonna make a run at him or drop him from here?" asked Stub.

"I think I can pick him off," said Caddo. "If I can't, we'll have to charge him."

As coldly as if sighting down his rifle at a deer, Caddo knelt and took his bead. Fuzz Knight was singing discordantly as the wagon rolled closer. The driver was no more than fifty yards away when Caddo pulled the trigger.

Fuzz did not drop right out of the seat. Caddo cursed, threw another shell into his rifle, shot again. Then he saw that his first bullet had hit center. Now Fuzz was slumped over the seat, head hanging from the wagon. The six mules clomped on stolidly. Caddo halted them by seizing the harness of the first pair.

Caddo searched Knight's pockets and exclaimed in delight at finding Anthony's thousand dollars.

"Luck's with us," he called out to Stubby.

Stubby was as pleased. "This beats skinning steers all hollow," agreed Wright. A man who had ridden with Quantrell did not relish such hard and dirty work as stripping dead cattle of their hides.

Caddo kicked the dead driver over the seat, then pulled him into the mesquite bushes.

"I'll be damned if I burn this wagon before we sell the tallow," he grinned. "Come on, we'll freight this ourselves."

Stubby Wright quickly agreed. The well trained mules followed the trail without coaching, and the wagon lumbered on to Port Isabel without incident. Stubby and Caddo took turns sleeping. The tallow made a soft bed even if it left a gruesome smell.

In Port Isabel they sold the wagon for a hundred dollars and the mules for twice as much. Without bills of sales to show, they felt they had made a good deal. The tallow was easy to dispose of. At Isabel were a dozen traders who brought tallow and hides without asking questions.

Caddo and his partner rode back to Alice with two thousand dollars remaining of their plunder, even after a spree in the coast town.

They reached Alice and reported to Marvin Sledge. The banker heard them with a leer.

"That should be something for Anthony to think about," Caddo grinned. "One thousand cash, a wagon, six mules, a load of tallow, and one dead driver. How long can he take that?"

"And the danged waddy is busy throwing a wedding for Melba Melvin and Fritz Warner?" chuckled Sledge. "There's a saying that a fool and his money are soon parted. Anthony is a fool for trying to buck me."

There would be an open house in the hotel after the wedding.

Music, whisky on the house, food, but everybody bring gifts for the bride and groom.

The ceremony itself was set for six o'clock. The happy couple would leave on the ten o'clock stage for San Antonio.

Bess Earnest rode in that afternoon, with two gifts for Melba.

"We decided not to come to the dance," she explained awkwardly.

Melba nodded, her lips tight. Naturally Walt Earnest didn't want to show his face.

"My dad will never forgive himself, Melba," Bess said pitifully. "Don't hold it against us."

"I'm not," Melba denied. "It's sweet of you to ride in, Elizabeth." Then, studying Bess's strained face: "I guess I can be returning the favor before long," she said, indicating the presents. "When are you and Harry gonna get hitched?"

She waited a little breathlessly for the answer. She had every reason to despise Harry Odell, but that didn't come easily.

"Perhaps in the spring," Bess said carelessly. Then, after a moment: "Is Ben in town?"

"Yes, over at the yard."

One woman can read another one. The expression on Bess Earnest's face came as a shock to Melba. After Bess had gone, the dark-haired girl stared out of the window a long time without seeing any of the rolling landscape. Was it life, she wondered, that a woman loved one man but married another one?

Bess did start across the street to Ben's wagon yard. Any number of times she had visited him in his small unpainted office, with no consciousness of being forward. But now, as she saw him leave the smithy and come toward his wagon shed, a spot showed in each cheek, and she slowed her steps.

Then she turned back altogether. For Harry Odell came riding by without seeing her, and she heard Ben hail him and saw her fiancé pull in his horse. She returned to Morgan Mann's store and, mounting her horse, rode away without speaking to either man. The day had passed when she could chat with them at the same time.

But there was no change in Ben Anthony's relations with Harry Odell. Certainly, after these days, both Harry and Bess had forgotten the one time Ben had permitted his emotions to leap out of their shackles.

"Why the glad rags?" Ben asked, noticing Harry's white shirt and flowing tie.

"They tell you're throwing a shindig for the bride and groom," grinned Harry. "What does a shindig in this country amount to without ol' Harry?"

Ben did not return his joviality. "I don't think you oughta show up, Harry," he said curtly.

To do Harry Odell credit, this was the first time he had been reminded of his relationship with Melba Melvin. He frowned, then nodded.

"I guess it ain't the thing to do," he sighed. He was disappointed. He had looked forward to a town dance.

"I'll buy a drink," he offered.

"No time," Ben refused.

"I'll grab one and ride on back," Harry said in a disgusted tone, as if it were unfair that a man's past always followed in his tracks, ruining his fun.

He hitched his horse in front of the saloon and strolled inside. Caddo Parker, who was playing solitaire, gave him a grin. Harry downed his drink and stepped outside. The outlaw followed. The street was deserted. Caddo leaned against a post picking his teeth with a broken-off match. Harry bent over and adjusted his stirrups. To the average eye it did not seem that the two men were speaking.

"How's your friend Anthony?" demanded Caddo. "Is he as salty as usual?"

"I guess. Why?"

"Thought mebbe he might be a little upset," grinned Caddo. "Or I guess he ain't found out that he's lost a wagonload of tallow, wagon and all. And a driver."

Harry looked up quickly. "Your work, Caddo?"

"You're always insinuating I'm crooked," sighed Caddo. "I just heard about it, that's all."

"If you did it," Harry growled, "God help you. You start fooling with Anthony's wagons, and he'll mop up this country with you. Take my word for it."

"He ain't scaring me none," jeered Caddo. "He's big, but I've seen a wasp chase a steer all over a section pasture."

93

9

Two riders from the Tall Y, forty miles down the Port Isabel road, brought the news to Anthony that his driver had been killed and his wagon stolen. Ben had begun to worry about Fuzz, who was now two days overdue.

"The coyotes had gotten to the body," explained one of the riders. "We dug a hole and shoveled dirt over him."

"Look around for tracks?" Ben asked sharply.

"Some. Best we could tell, a couple of guys did it. They tied their mounts behind the wagon and drove on."

Ben nodded. Early next morning he rode to the spot of the crime. There was nothing beyond that the riders had furnished him: a grave, a man shot twice by a rifle, wagon tracks leading on to Port Isabel. Ben rode on to the coast city. But he could discover no trace of his wagon. Riding back, he searched for evidence that his wagon had turned off the road. He could find no sign.

When he returned to Alice, Melba and Fritz Warner had returned from San Antonio, and had already taken up housekeeping on Fritz's small ranch.

"Melba seem happy?" he asked Tommy, who supplied the information.

Tommy shot him a sharp look. Was there anything behind this question?

"I guess," he murmured. "Find out anything about the wagon?"

"No."

Tommy studied his employer. "Shifty was due in today," he said quietly. "Do you reckon . . ."

Ben was already fagged out from his trip to Isabel, but he took the saddle and the San Antonio road. Fifteen miles from Alice he located tracks leading off the trail. Five hundred yards away, in a wooded flat, he found the charred remains of his wagon, and the corpse of Shifty Pendleton, thus named for his wavering eyesight. The mules had been slaughtered.

Wagon and merchandise had been burned. Ben recalled this shipment. A thousand dollars' worth of leather goods and staple groceries in addition to the cost of the wagon and mules!

He fairly quivered with rage. This was worse, in his eyes, than the loss of the load of tallow. For here robbery had not been the motive at all, but ruthless slaughter. He dug a grave for Shifty, threw dirt over the mule carcasses, and returned to Alice.

He broke the grave news to Morgan Mann. They had accepted the first theft as an overdue dose of bad luck. With so many unemployed riders around, it was not unexpected that a hard-pressed pair would seize the opportunity to stage a holdup, drive the wagon and tallow on to Port Isabel, and clean up a grubstake. But this wanton slaughter, and burning!

Caddo Parker had regretted it, if that was to the outlaw's credit. But Caddo did not dare attempt to drive the wagon along by-trails to where he could turn back onto the *Camino Real* without fear of apprehension. He and Stubby had carried off what they could pack on their saddles, and set fire to the rest.

Morgan's broad face was grim. "I reckon they're out to freeze us out, Ben," he growled. "I didn't think Marvin Sledge would get that low."

"You think it's Marvin?"

"Who else would be interested? Caddo now, he'd steal the ring off his dead grandmother's finger. But Caddo ain't just burning wagons and killing drivers for the hell of it. Somebody is footing the bill, and I'll bet my Sunday boots it's Sledge."

Ben nodded, pulled on his hat, and strode toward the saloon. It was midafternoon, and the usual crowd of jobless riders was there. Ben called all hands outside. Even Caddo Parker followed.

"Men," Ben announced, "I'm hiring guards for my wagons and stages. I can use four men to each wagon. The pay ain't too much, and you'll have to do some shooting. How's fifty a month and keep?"

Some of these men were already riding with Caddo Parker. The dark-bearded outlaw watched the reaction with a thin grin.

Ben succeeded in hiring twelve guards. The others gave various excuses for not taking up this offer.

These laggards earned Ben's tongue-lashing. "You men have gotten by here because there was no work to be had," he said coldly. "I've fed some of you myself, and nobody even wrote it down. The day of free meals is over at my restaurant. And you men who can keep on hanging around, buying your share of drinks and playing poker, might be asked some straight questions. You'd better have the answers ready."

"Sure," Caddo jeered. "Ben Anthony is a one-man law force. No need for the Rangers with Anthony around, a tough guy like him."

This was their first direct clash. Ben climbed down from the hitching rail.

"I never make talk about being tough, Caddo," he said slowly. "But get any notion that this country is afraid of you out of your head. My wagons are going through. These ranchmen are going to get tired of losing stock. We've had tougher hombres than you to deal with, and smarter. If you want to keep your health, Parker, you'll make tracks."

Caddo laughed hoarsely. "I'll be in this town after you're gone, Anthony."

And he took a step forward, unafraid. He wore his guns low, held in their holsters by a clip. Confidence was written on his dark face. He had faced other men who were considered swift and deadly with a gun, and he was still riding.

Ben studied the outlaw a moment, suddenly aware that the moment for fight was here. The enmity had been there all along, quick and founded on nothing more than the challenge one strong man feels for another. But here was the fight. Here Caddo stood, leaning forward slightly, hands slightly crooked at the elbows.

Ben realized he was not Caddo's equal with a six-gun. He realized without a qualm of fear that he was not a six-gun man. He was a crack shot with a rifle, but he had never spent hours practicing and mastering the intricacies of a quick draw.

"I don't play your way, Caddo," he murmured. "I'm no fancy gunman. I'm ready for you. But, if you say the word, and I take you on, don't be surprised at how I fight."

Caddo's lips curled. Already in this new country was springing up a breed of fighting men. They laughed at the code of honor of the country they had left behind them, but here, on this frontier, in less than a generation, they had adopted another. Caddo laughed as scornfully as a New Orleans dandy of a half-century before would have laughed at a skin-clad woodsman from Kentucky who refused a silver-mounted dueling pistol.

"Thought you were grown up, Anthony," he sneered. "What do you carry that gun for, an ornament?"

Ben did not answer, except to take a step forward. The outlaw's hands dropped lower.

"You don't get a hand on me, Anthony," he warned. "I'll give you credit for having the strength of a grizzly. Take another step and I'll—"

He was interrupted by Harry Odell's sudden arrival on horseback. Odell threw his reins over the post and quickly sized up the situation.

"What's up?" he demanded.

"Me and your friend, Anthony," sneered Caddo, "are having a little argument."

"Stay out of it, Harry," Ben snapped. He took another half-step, cautious, tense. He had to get as close as he could before Caddo make a jerk at his gun. He had to be close enough to be in on Parker before Caddo could whip that gun up.

Harry caught his friend's arm. "Here, let it go," he said. "I want to talk to you."

"Later," Ben said, shaking clear.

Harry stepped squarely between them. "There's no fight today," he declared.

Caddo raised his hands. The dark-faced outlaw was surprised at his own relief, and confused. He had been so sure that he could face any man in the world, and that no man walking slowly toward him with the intention of fighting him barehanded would have frightened him. But he found himself glad that Harry Odell had intervened, and that Ben Anthony seemed willing to accept the postponement. For that was all it was. Caddo knew it. Anthony knew it. Odell knew it.

"Come inside for a drink," urged Harry.

Ben followed. No jeer came from Caddo's lips. Ben Anthony had not been afraid, and Caddo knew it. Caddo turned to the hitching rack without a word, mounted his horse, and rode toward Falfurrias. He was more shaken than he liked to admit. He didn't like what he knew, that Anthony was willing to walk into the face of a gun.

Harry insisted on Ben's having another before he mentioned the trouble he had interrupted.

"Getting ambitious?" he asked. "Parker is known to be muy malo with a six-gun."

Ben explained that he had lost two wagons. "I don't mind a man stealing so much," he said. "But killing a driver and my mules, and burning the freight right there—a guy who'll do that doesn't deserve to live."

Harry's brain was beating like a trip hammer. Caddo must be doing this with Sledge's approval. Even Sledge's cooperation. And neither had mentioned to him a campaign to ruin Ben Anthony.

He listened, and fury burned in his own heart. He had been quick to put in a word that would sour Elizabeth Earnest against his boyhood friend, but that had been because Anthony threatened something which Harry considered as his own. His friendship never extended to giving up his own possessions. But, in his strange way, Harry Odell was loyal to Ben Anthony as well as aware of the big man's force. It was difficult to know where loyalty left off and fear began.

He listened, and cold sweat gleamed on his forehead. For Anthony said, in a calm tone:

"I guess it's up to me to run Caddo out of here. I've hired twelve men to guard my wagons. I won't ask 'em to go after Caddo, just to shoot if he jumps them. But I think this country is tired of Caddo and his steer skinners. I'll ride out and talk to Walt in the morning."

The damned fools, Harry thought, cursing Sledge and Parker. Between them they could have crushed every other man in this country. But they had to challenge the one person who had the capital to fight Sledge's bank and the strength to fight Caddo's guns!

He left Ben as quickly as he could find an excuse and thundered into Sledge's private office.

"You've played hell!" he snarled. "What ever gave you the notion to turn Caddo loose on Anthony's wagons?"

"Anthony is in our way," Sledge said coldly. "We'll ruin him within six months."

"Yeah! Why wasn't I asked about this? What are you trying to do—doublecross *me*?"

"Neither Caddo nor I thought it was any of your affair," Sledge shot back.

Harry snorted. "I'll make it my affair. I'm not fighting Anthony, Sledge. If that's in the game, you can deal me out."

"You're in too far to quit," the banker said coldly. "There's one way out for you, Odell, and only one. Caddo will attend to that if I say the word."

Harry's face paled, and his anger ebbed. So that was it? He was held fast in their clutches.

He stared at Sledge. It was new to Harry Odell to have another man tell him what to do. But Sledge would. And did.

"This isn't a boys' game, Odell," the banker went on in that same merciless tone. "I told you that before you pitched in. I have my plans. Ben Anthony is no personal concern of mine. He's a friend of yours, and I'm sorry we have to ruin him. Don't let your friendship for Anthony worry you too much, Odell. Just figger it's the way the cards are running, and let it go at that. Because Caddo Parker will handle you just as he will handle Anthony if you don't."

Harry paled. This was no idle threat, and he knew it. He muttered something and stalked away, angry with Anthony, angry with Sledge, angry with himself.

For Harry Odell was disturbed by what Caddo Parker and Marvin Sledge were not—a fear of their failure. He could have reconciled Anthony's ruin, and Anthony's inevitable death, with his conscience. Harry's conscience was as pliable as a hemp rope.

But that fear of failure, that premonition of doom! It was childish for one grown man to believe another so invulnerable. Harry Odell, who chid Ben Anthony for not knowing the way to kiss a girl, who passed on a rumor discrediting him even when he knew that rumor was false, did not believe Caddo Parker, or anyone else, would kill Ben Anthony. Ben had his limitations, and Harry knew these better than any other man. But the ability to survive was not one of them. Caddo was fast with a six-gun and sure, and logical reasoning gave the outlaw an edge. But Harry Odell was never logical.

Failure would ruin him, for failure would bring exposure. Harry galloped back to his house and opened another bottle of whisky. He sat and drank until his head dropped forward on his chest, and he was dead to the world. Damn Sledge and Parker! Damn Anthony! Why had Ben formed this partnership with Morgan Mann!

Again Harry Odell must scheme his way out of a corner. For he did not seriously consider for a moment that Caddo Parker would conquer big Ben Anthony. Harry Odell believed in nothing as firmly as he did in Ben's power to survive all physical threats.

Some of Harry's confidence had returned with morning. He cooked his own breakfast, for his three vaqueros were already out on the Dollar Mark range. He never wasted a thought on how fortunate he was to have such dependable riders. They were slow, they were inexpert, but they were faithful. Without them the Dollar Mark ranch would have been in deplorable condition.

After dinner he rode toward Walt Earnest's, still undecided as to what he could do next. Walt had not heard of Ben's run-in with Caddo Parker.

Harry described it after supper. He could see in the gathering twilight that Elizabeth Earnest was disturbed. Inside him, a voice laughed harshly. If only he could be sure that Caddo Parker would carry out his threat and shoot Ben Anthony down in some kind of fight! Bess had never mentioned that kiss by the well, but now her expression changed whenever Ben's name was mentioned. And Harry referred to his friend often, watching her slyly at each mention.

"Well," Walt Earnest said finally, "I can't say I'm sorry."

"Dad!" exclaimed Bess reproachfully. "You know this Parker's reputation. And you know Ben won't back down. He'll walk right into Caddo's gun."

"And break Caddo in two with his own bare hands," Walt said fiercely. "Don't waste your sympathy on Ben Anthony, girl. Pity, instead, the man who tries to stand up against him."

Harry Odell nodded. He felt that way. It sounded absurd, but he was glad someone else was sure of it, too.

"I can't still see why you're glad it happened," Elizabeth snapped.

"We've been needing a fight," Walt Earnest said dreamily, staring off over his ranch. "It's been coming for two years. Seems like this country gets itself into such a shape every now and then that nothing but a good fight will straighten it out. I've been feeling in my bones for some time that I would be in it. I also got a hunch it'll be my last one. I want Ben Anthony on my side when it comes."

"Wouldn't he have been anyhow?" Elizabeth asked softly.

Walt's lips curved in a smile, and he gnawed on the tips of his mustaches. "Sure," he said after a moment. "I raised a boy there."

Melba Melvin made no pretense to happiness. She had accepted Fritz Warner, and she was living with him in the two-room cabin which looked down upon Odell's Dollar Mark ranch. Perhaps if the white Odell house had not been constantly before her eyes she would have been more satisfied. Each glimpse brought back the memory of Harry, and of their moments together; and stolid industrious Fritz suffered in comparison.

Fritz was a dull man. His was a dull life. He was at work at dawn, which meant cooking his breakfast in the chill dark, and packing him a lunch in a tin pail, for he did not wish to waste the time required to ride back home. He was in late, and by the time he had wolfed his meal with the appetite of a famished man it was bedtime again. It was an empty frugal life, and Melba had had an overdose of both emptiness and frugality. She wanted ease, and a little laughter: ease and laughter and affection instead of grim duty; the life of a Harry Odell or a Bess Earnest. Fritz owned his land and his cattle while her father had possessed neither, but otherwise Fritz Warner could have been Timothy Melvin, answering each urge of youth with the sour "We can't afford it" or "We can't waste the time."

But there was a difference between Fritz Warner and her father as men. Once when she had complained, Fritz told her with some pride: "It will not always be so. I am getting ahead. Soon I can hire a rider. I have cut mesquite and cactus out of my creek valley. Already I can feed more cattle to the acre than Walt Earnest."

Once she rode with him and sat and watched while he worked. Every spare minute was spent clearing mesquite and cactus. Melba sighed as she looked at the immensity of the task, even on a place as small as his. Could one man clear mesquite and cactus quicker than they could grow back?

He had his promises, and he told her about them shyly, and pieces at a time. But she listened only impatiently. What he promised was in the dim future, and the girl Melba had decided recklessly to live in the present. Fritz held out no gay present. He knew nothing of gayety, and thus was not lonely for it. Never having had any complaints himself, he did not know how to deal with them. All he had ever asked was the right to work with his own two hands, and to know that no man could seize what he had so laboriously pieced together.

Melba had been trained to diligence; but her self-pity mounted, and her husband's stolid indifference to her complaints magnified them in her eyes. Why had she listened to Ben Anthony and taken this animal for a husband? Yes, it was Anthony's persuasion. Perhaps, if she had not acted so hastily, she still could have had Harry Odell. Haunting her was the recollection of Bess Earnest's face when the ranchman's daughter asked about Ben Anthony and went out of the hotel to seek him, knowing that she went on no routine matter, but to see a man she loved. Melba brooded over this. Why couldn't Bess Earnest have Ben Anthony? Then Harry Odell would be left for her. And, without Bess, she could have him. Harry had found her desirable, and that was a form of love. Better than what Fritz was providing.

She took to riding over the country for hours at a time, running Fritz's saddle horse until the bay animal was lathered with sweat and suffered from swollen forelegs. Patiently Fritz explained that he did not work this mare on the range because she was of blooded stock, of Morgan Steeldust strain, and he wished to keep her for a brood mare. By breeding her to other Quarterhorse thoroughbreds, he would build up a string of good horses against the day his spreading ranch would need them. And a colt by a fine stallion, out of such a mare, would be worth $150 more than many steers. Melba stubbornly continued her rides. With a sigh Fritz yielded. He must yield everything to this dark-eyed stormy girl who took so contemptuously what he offered. But then Fritz had behind him a lifetime of giving up to others; it was not so hard. His sort could only make the most of what was there, and go plodding ahead.

Melba at first had no desire to see Harry Odell face to face; instead, she felt a horror of that inevitable time when they must meet. But, with the passing days, her fears ebbed. When she rode away from Warner's small cottage she could see either the Odell house or the Odell vaqueros. Sometimes there was a fourth rider; she knew this must be Harry himself, and goose bumps popped out all over her flesh, and inevitably she turned the bay mare toward home, only to wheel about and ride still closer, hanging to the shelter of screening ridges.

Several times Odell saw a rider silhouetted against the sky for a brief moment, but always at such a distance that he did not recognize his former sweetheart. Four outfits overflowed into these flats; he guessed the rider to be a Maitland or a Cameron.

Then, one afternoon, Melba came close enough for him to see the flash of scarlet around her throat. He dropped his branding iron with a chuckle and turned toward his horse. He had made his promise to Ben Anthony in all sincerity—no more playing around with women until he had married Elizabeth Earnest. But it never occurred to him again. The flash of scarlet was a challenge any time, more so since circumstances threw the odds against him. It would be fun to sweet-talk her around to his way again.

Melba whirled the bay as she saw him mounting, and was off at a dead run. She rode better than the average woman, and Fritz's mare was of Quarterhorse strain, quick as a flash for a short distance. She galloped back to the cottage and, as if in shame-faced repentance for what she had thought, baked fresh rolls for supper that evening. Fritz came in, weary and uncommunicative, and made no mention of the delicacy. Melba's bosom swelled in defiance. She should have known better than to waste her time trying to appeal to this stolid German.

The next day she looked down upon Harry and his vaqueros from a ridge two miles away.

Now he was beginning to watch for her. He was out earlier with his riders, and more faithfully. For three days she was only a speck in the distance.

"Damn her," said Harry with a chuckle, "I'll teach her to tease a man."

He carried his vaqueros into the south pasture, farther away from Fritz Warner's cottage. He watched to see if Melba would follow. For a day he had no sign of her, and he cursed impatiently. Then, near noon of the second day, she swung in sight across the mesquite slopes, and he mounted his horse and turned toward Alice, as if he had not seen her.

But, once over the ridge, he dug spurs into his mount and doubled back in a wide loop. Unless she had turned at once and was riding hell-bent for election, he would intercept her.

Melba heard the hoofs ahead, but was unsuspecting. The Maitlands and the Camerons used this trail; it could be any of them. Besides, she had seen Odell ride toward town.

He heard her coming and pulled up behind a tall cactus clump. He spurred his horse out into the trail just ahead of her, and, as her horse shied, caught its bridle.

Melba had not jerked or spurred the horse away. Her hands had dropped from the reins, involuntarily, and she sat frozen in the saddle, for the moment incapable of motion.

"Danged if you're not as pretty as ever!" murmured Harry appreciatively. The riding and the wind did that to her coloring—deepened it, richened it.

Now he climbed out of the saddle, still holding her bridle. He looked up at her with the grin she had come to despise.

"I've missed you," he said. "How is Fritz treating you?"

Now Melba recovered control of her reflexes. She jerked the bridle from his hands, dug spurs into the flanks of the bay mare, and raced for the security of Fritz's cottage.

Fritz heard the thundering of the mare's hoofs, and sighed. One should not run such a valuable mare across such uneven ground. Any kind of bog hole, any kind of mesquite root, and down would go the bay with a broken leg.

Harry Odell looked after the fleeing girl with a grin, and a shrug of his shoulders. So she was afraid of him! Harry was wise enough as far as women were concerned to realize that this was in his favor. She couldn't stay out of his sight, and yet she was afraid to be near him.

It occurred to him that Fritz Warner might see them from any high ridge, by accident or by design. He shrugged his shoulders again.

In some ways Harry Odell could be more reckless than Caddo Parker or Ben Anthony.

10

Ben Anthony studied his accounts and reported the bad news to his partner.

"We can't last much longer at this rate, Morgan," he said grimly. "We've lost ten thousand dollars' worth of merchandise, wagons, and mules in the last two weeks. Not to mention our drivers."

Morgan Mann nodded glumly. No firm could survive this rain of holdups.

"I've got to replace those wagons," Ben said. "I need at least three to keep up with the King deliveries."

A wagon train was scheduled to start out through Duval County, carrying supplies to four big outfits Morgan had solicited business from. Morgan mentioned this.

"Those wagons have to get through," he said. "They're depending on us. They need those supplies bad, Ben. The Broad Arrow ain't had flour in a week."

Ben nodded. "I'll carry that myself. I'll take six guards. We'll fight off Caddo's wolves."

"How about the wagons?"

"I'll send Tommy to Port Isabel," Ben decided. "On horseback. Then I'll double back there and join him. Wait four days, then send the other six guards to Isabel."

"You can't ride every wagon going out of here, Ben," Morgan shrugged.

The big man had been doing just that. Night and day he had been on the trail since the holdups had broken out. Twice they had scared off attacks by sheer weight of numbers. Caddo Parker could lay his hands on any number of men who would skin steers for a few dollars, but not many cared to attack freight wagons protected by straight-shooting guards.

Ben drew three thousand dollars out of the bank. The wagons and mules would cost more, but, if Tommy reached his agents in Isabel, his account would be good for the rest.

Sledge made a mental note of the withdrawal, and promptly summoned Parker. "I reckon you can use that three thousand," he grinned at the bearded outlaw.

"Got a place for it," nodded Parker. "Who's carrying it? Where to? What for?"

"Anthony forgot to tell me," shrugged Sledge.

"Now that was plumb forgetful of him," grinned Parker. "That means I'll have to ride herd on his wagon yard."

He assigned a new recruit, who had ridden with the Tipton gang on the border, to this chore. Red Riley reported back that afternoon that the kid who acted as loading foreman—Melvin or something—was leaving, going southwest, and that Anthony himself was taking out three wagons with six guards.

Caddo Parker mulled over the prospects. Anthony was probably heading out with merchandise to be delivered; several heavily guarded wagons had come into Alice from Isabel, and Anthony's crews had done considerable unloading and reloading.

"Let's tail the Melvin button," he told Riley and Stubby Wright.

"We'll have to take off like a sage hen," said Red. "He was riding single, and he's fanning the breeze."

"How much of a start?" frowned Caddo.

"An hour anyways."

"Riding single?"

"Yes."

"We'll take extra horses," decided Caddo. "We can run him down."

"Sounds like a badger chase to me," grumbled Stubby, who did not relish the job ahead.

"I'm giving the order," snapped Caddo. He never tolerated indecision or insubordination from his men.

The three took the trail, each man carrying an extra horse. Every hour, they changed. The extra horses were also saddled, they lost no time.

Still they couldn't overtake Tommy Melvin. The youngster was riding hard, conscious of the responsibility Ben Anthony had thrusted onto his shoulders.

It was not until dark, twenty miles or more from Alice, that Caddo Parker sighted the rider ahead. He threw up his rifle and took a quick shot as Tommy, hearing the pursuit, veered off the trail.

"Now you've done it!" said Riley in disgust. "Now we'll have to smoke him out of these hills."

"We would have anyhow," said Caddo. Lately Ben's men were shooting on sight, and Caddo's work was as dangerous as it ever had been.

Tommy had sighted the three men behind him, each leading a spare mount, and realized instantly he was being chased. His horse was tired under him, and he knew he couldn't make a run for it. He turned his mount into the mesquite just as Caddo's bullet sailed over his head. Turning, he shot from a standstill. His bullet made the outlaws scatter, but the range was too far by at least two hundred yards. He pulled his horse into the shelter of a cactus bed and waited. Seeing Caddo ride through the brushy flat below him, he pumped two swift shots at the dark-bearded outlaw. Neither did any damage. Tommy cursed and reloaded. He wished he had the accuracy of Ben Anthony with a rifle. Never had the Melvin finances permitted extensive practice— shells came too high. Besides, Timothy Melvin had never liked to have his boys shoot guns.

A bullet whined above Tommy's head; he threw himself from his horse. The shot had come from behind. Red Riley and Stubby Wright had gone to work swiftly, and expertly. Hunting down a man in the brush was an old story to them. Caddo directed them with waves of his hand, and quickly Tommy was surrounded.

The youngster sensed his fate. There were three against him, and he had no illusions about his ability to outshoot them. He unsaddled his horse with fumbling fingers, slapped the animal on the rump and shouted, "Git!" Then, pulling his saddle a few yards, he took out the cash and tossed it into the cactus bed. And, in the sand, with a forked stick, wrote:

"Caddo Parker and two men. Trailed me from Alice. Cactus."

Then, darting low through the mesquite, Tommy sought another spot. He had unsaddled his horse because often an unsaddled pony knows enough to hit the trail home. He had left a clear trail. Anthony, he knew, would come after him. Anthony would find the saddle, with the money, and the writing in the sand.

Now he had to work his three assailants away from the spot where he had written, and where the money was hidden. He saw that his horse grazed uncertainly a moment, then began drifting back up the trail. He prayed that the animal would have the judgment to strike out for home.

A bullet whined close to him, but he kept running. He reached a shale ridge and there stretched out at full length. Not for a moment did he kid himself about his chances of fighting off these outlaws. But he had protected Anthony's money to the best of his power. He had left in the sand the incriminating evidence that would send Anthony after Caddo Parker; and he had the same opinion of the big man's physical powers as Harry Odell.

In the gathering dusk, as Caddo and his two killers crept closer, Tommy Melvin unbuttoned his belt and piled his shells before him. He could put up a fight. He had come of a breed that was not supposed to fight. A nester was supposed to turn and run. But the Melvins had never been real squatter people. Timothy Melvin hadn't been.

Tommy rolled a cigarette. He was proud of the sureness of his fingers, of his wet lips as he licked the paper. He sighted a movement in the brush and threw his gun to his shoulder. The faint cry of pain brought a grin to his young face.

He wished Ben could see him like this, cigarette in mouth, rifle ready.

"You'll get me," he said grimly, to the empty grayness creeping over the ridges. "But you'll have Ben Anthony after you. You'll see the day you wish you'd never jumped me."

For two days Melba did not leave the Warner house. For two days she damned Harry Odell with the fury of a woman who has been taken lightly, who has had her weaknesses thrown back into her face. And there is no other fury comparable to this.

But on the third day she ventured forth again. This time she wore a new blouse she had bought in San Antonio, one that was daring for the country and the time. Harry caught a glimpse of her over a mile away, but continued his work with a grin. This handsome man had been born with a gift for handling women, and some men. The fact that she came back indicated that she wanted to see him again. Harry was wise enough to know that there was a time to chase, and a time to keep his distance. He could play a woman as a wise poker player plays a hand.

On the fourth day Melba ventured even closer. Harry dropped his branding iron, mounted his horse, and rode slowly toward her. She saw him coming, waited a moment, then turned and started toward home. But her pace permitted quick overtaking.

Harry came up beside her.

"You're as hard to catch as a coyote," he grinned.

Melba did not answer. The bay mare continued its slow pace. Harry caught the bridle.

"You don't run away from me again," he chuckled.

He hadn't been sure of her at first. But now he knew that marriage to Fritz Warner hadn't changed her feeling for him.

"What do you want, Harry?" she asked bitterly.

"To look at you—first," he answered. "Then—a kiss."

She looked off and then back, eyes coated with a film of defiance. "You seem to forget I'm married."

"I've never forgotten it," he said. "I've never understood why."

"What else was there for me? I came to you, didn't I?"

There was an appealing note in her voice. And she was not asking him for mercy. She was appealing to somebody else, somewhere else. Perhaps Melba Melvin Warner knew herself, and was asking for help against herself.

Harry slid from the saddle and caught her hand. "Come on down," he smiled.

"No," she answered curtly.

His pressure tightened. "Come on. The bay needs a rest anyhow."

"No," she repeated.

But, even as she uttered the negative, she knew she would. His hand pulled her, and she obeyed.

Standing on her feet, her eyes meeting his firmly, she straightened her blouse.

"Well," she said. "I'm down."

"Yes," he smiled. "You're down."

She stood straight and stiff under his smile, glaring at him, hating him for the confidence of his grin and his look, yet knowing that she was still subject to his desires.

"I thought you'd miss me," he murmured, gripping her shoulder. "I didn't think you could marry that Bohunk and never give a damn about what happened to ol' Harry."

Melba did not answer. Harry's arm tightened around her, and he pulled her closer.

"Haven't you got a kiss for a man you haven't seen in days?" he coaxed.

She made no movement toward him, but neither did she present any resistance. Harry's arm went even tighter, and he tilted up her chin with his fingers.

"You're a sweet girl," he said huskily. "I was a fool to give you up. You're worth any range anywhere."

She hated him for saying that, but she did not stop him. There was nothing of her old flaming love in her surrender. Hers was a mute acceptance of his will again. But she tasted nothing of his sweetness in his kiss, only bitterness, only restlessness. Not for a moment did she doubt that she had come to hate him.

He lifted her off her feet, and she looked up at him with a veiled light in her eyes that Harry Odell mistook for something else. Harry could not be expected to understand such a surrender. A woman, at times, is capable of things a man can never expect, because a man has never known them. Melba Melvin finally closed her eyes, and sighed. Why did it take this to show her what she should have known all along?

An hour later Harry pulled his hat over his eyes and kissed her lightly on the cheek.

"I got to get back," he murmured. "When are you going to ride this way again?"

"Never," she said curtly.

He was taken aback by her tone. Damn her, she seemed to actually mean that! What was she trying to pull on him!

Then he chuckled. She would be back. "Oh, you'll get lonesome and come around," he grinned. "Better get home and cook the Bohunk's supper. They tell me he eats like a horse."

Melba sat up and began straightening her hair. He looked down from the saddle at her. There was nothing of embarrassment in her answering gaze. And yet nothing of the old helplessness she had felt before him.

Neither noticed that, halfway up the slope and no more than a hundred yards away, Fritz Warner had reined up his horse and was watching with a set look of his own.

"Next time," Harry said lightly, "we'll ride over to the house. You've never seen my house, have you?"

"I don't want to," Melba muttered.

Harry laughed softly and touched spurs to his horse. A man learns to look for surprises from a woman. Let her act peeved and stand-offish if she wanted to. The next time he saw her, and wanted her, it would be the same.

As he rode off, Fritz Warner also turned his horse and went slowly back to his own cedar fence. The stray calf he had been searching for was permitted to wander unchallenged. For the moment, Fritz had more on his mind than a stray calf.

Melba suddenly was in motion. She burst into tears and fairly leaped into the saddle. Her blouse was askew and her riding skirt was soiled, but she did not care. Nor did she finish rearranging her hair. She spurred the bay mare into a wild run, and raced it until its sides heaved from exhaustion. The Morgan Steeldust strain was not bred for durability, and the mare was breathing wheezily after a half-mile.

The wind whipped Melba's long black hair, she had left her kerchief on the ground. Flying pebbles stung her face. But still the mare couldn't go fast enough. Once it stumbled, but Melba whipped her on unrelentingly.

But suddenly she pulled the mare down to a slow trot. Suddenly, as if his voice had sounded right in her ear, she recalled Fritz Warner's pleas not to mistreat this horse, not to risk a broken leg, or a strained muscle. Suddenly she remembered that this was Fritz's brood mare, and hers. Nothing must happen to this horse. This was a pure-blood Morgan Steeldust, and bred to a thoroughbred would produce fine range ponies. Later, when his ranch had grown, he would need a remuda for the hands he would hire.

It was near dark when she reached the corral. Supper should

be on the table. But she took the time to rub down the mare, and curry its soft mane. She gave the horse a double ration of oats and pressed her face against the still perspiring neck.

"From now on," she sobbed, "I'll be good to you. I'll treat you like a baby."

Then she ran for the house. Fritz would be in soon, and there must be a hot meal ready for him such as he had never eaten before. Of course he had the appetite of a horse. Why shouldn't he? He worked like one.

But darkness dropped over the swelling ridges, and still no Fritz. The steak she had fried cooled. The boiled potatoes ceased to steam. The coffee she finally poured herself was luke-warm and had to be reheated.

As she was stirring her cup, Fritz entered. One look at his face, and she knew something had happened. She could guess what.

Who couldn't have seen them—right out in the middle of the wide-open prairie?

"You're late, Fritz," she said gently.

"Yes," he said in a monotone, "I am late."

She waited a moment. He stood a step over the doorway, looking at her in an absorbed way, as if he were seeing beyond her.

"Did you work hard?" she asked nervously, turning from him to the stove, throwing fresh kindling under the potatoes and steak.

"Yes."

"Sit down, and I'll pour you coffee before we eat. It's already hot."

He came forward another pace, slowly, reluctantly. His face was dark in the wavering lamplight. Melba shot him a sudden shy look. It was strange to feel shy before him. Yes, he must know. She poured a cup of coffee and motioned him to the table.

"Sit down, Fritz."

He did not move. Nor, for a moment, did he answer. She saw his fingernails biting into the palms of his hands. She saw the unhappiness spread from his eyes all over his dark face.

"I can't sit," he said after a long moment. "There is nothing here for me. What is here belongs to another man."

Melba took his arm. "Sit down, Fritz," she said. "Sit down and drink your coffee."

He sat down, but he made no gesture toward the coffee. He sat with his back toward her, and she was glad to have it so. She could better say what she intended to say if she was not looking at him.

"Fritz," she asked. "Why did you marry me?"

He did not answer.

"You knew what I had been to Harry Odell," she added, self-indictment in her voice. "You knew that I was no good, the flighty daughter of a nester shot down for skinning cattle."

Fritz raised his head. "I never believed that about your father," he said grimly. "Your father was a good man."

"Yes," Melba softly agreed. "A good man. I didn't inherit his goodness, Fritz. I suppose you know—about—"

"You and Odell? Yes. I've seen you ride toward his range, Melba. It hurt worse—to know you were out seeking him?"

"I couldn't stay away, Fritz."

Her voice fell off. The words she had rehearsed didn't come from her lips at all.

"I went to him, Fritz," she murmured. The admission didn't hurt. It seemed to do her good to tell him so. "I went to him like any cheap hussy. For days he has been all I could think about. I tried to keep within these walls, and to remember what I had committed myself to. But something pulled me over—to his range—to where he could see me—close enough to where he would come after me. I knew he would come, Fritz. I knew he was that type of man."

Fritz looked up with a nod. Yes, Odell would follow her. Odell was certainly that breed.

"I'm glad I went, Fritz," Melba continued in that same gentle voice. "I couldn't stand it here—before. Something within me cried out against it. I felt I had been forced to marry you, and to come with you out here. I felt I was being held here by a pair of strong cruel arms. I found myself hating you. I found myself wishing I were dead. But now . . ."

A brief hush. Then she went on, a smile curving her lips. "I'm glad you saw us, Fritz. For I would have had to tell you. It saves me the trouble of explaining—how I feel—now. You're a man,

Fritz. You're a good man. I know how men feel about women—who do things like that. There'll be no more rides . . . to see Harry Odell . . . or any other man. I know what I want now, Fritz. I want this home. This ranch. This life before us, this life full of hard work and penny pinching until we can afford the things we want."

Fritz Warner bent his head. She made an awkward motion toward him, and her hand fell heavily on his shoulder. "Is it too late, Fritz?" she asked gently. It was not a plea, not a whimper. It was a question. "I don't know about these things. I only know that I hope—I pray—it isn't."

Now she had said all she could. Now she could only wait for his answer, and she was not surprised that it was slow in coming. This was a question no man could answer in a rush, except in the rush of an anger that was not yet soothed by a woman's frank honest appeal.

She waited stoically. She waited with features composed, with eyes calm.

Fritz raised his eyes, and Melba shrank back. She saw hardness there, and she was a little frightened. This range mocked at the silent man who challenged only the forces of nature around him, never the force of his fellow man. Melba had shared that opinion, that here was a man who would not fight. Now she knew better. Now she could only hope that none of that hatred was for her.

"I have been pushed too far," he said slowly. "Always people have made fun of me. Perhaps they are laughing now. Anthony maybe, though I think not. Odell certainly. And others."

He looked down at his gnarled twisted hands with a sigh. "I have done the best I could," he went on in that low strained tone. "I have never bothered any man. I have let men get the best of me. For that I was wrong. I set too high a value on material things. I yielded in all matters except those. I was trying to buy the respect that men did not give me on first sight, and women never at all."

He twisted his fingers until the muscles in his hands showed white.

"None of that will be so again," he said grimly. "There are some men who must be shown that Fritz Warner is a man himself, and able to fight for and hold what is his own."

She shrank back from the darkness of his mood. She had not expected this, this overwhelming torrent of frustration and hate, of determination. His eyes upon her were black savage pools, with no hint of a softening color. He leaned forward, and Melba recoiled another step.

But suddenly he reached for his coffee and held the cup with a steady hand while he tasted it.

He frowned. He handed the cup to her, and a smile broke across his face. She had never seen him really smile before.

"It is cold," he said gently. "Better you should heat it again."

11

Tommy Melvin's horse was in the wagon yard when Ben Anthony returned from Duval County. Francisco, one of the Mexican loaders, motioned to it.

"She come back," Francisco said in broken English. "No saddle. No Tommy."

Ben swung into the saddle without stopping for rest and took the road to Port Isabel. Though the trail was five days old, he found where Tommy had taken to the ridges. He found where Tommy had stripped off the saddle and written his incriminating message in the sand. A mile away, half hidden in a thicket, he found Tommy's body. A handful of shells lay around him, indicating that he hadn't finished his fight. He lay on his face; Ben turned him over gently and saw that a bullet in his forehead had caused his death.

Walking in a circle, Ben found the tracks of Caddo Parker, Red Riley, and Stubby Wright. He also found something else— a mound of fresh dirt. Evidently Tommy Melvin had taken a toll of his attackers.

Ben returned to the youth's corpse. What a loyal little button he was! Even under fire, even when looking death in the face, he had thought about Ben Anthony's money, and had taken a chance that Caddo Parker wouldn't follow his back trail.

Anthony buried his young helper, then rode back to Alice. This was an open-and-shut case of murder! Tommy's message in the sand would be taken as evidence by any jury. But the law in Jim Wells County was less than helpless, it was not even functioning. No outfit paid county taxes in these hungry years. The courthouse was closed except for the clerk's office, and Sheriff Jess Allman was eking out an existence on a small Duval spread.

"What could I do, Ben?" sighed the Sheriff when Anthony demanded Caddo's arrest, and trial. "I ain't got a deputy. I don't get paid myself."

"I'll furnish the deputies," Ben said grimly.

"Furthermore," Jess continued, "there's some doubt I got the authority to arrest anybody. We should have had an election last summer. We skipped it because who wanted to run for jobs that didn't carry pay? Mebbe my term of office is over, I dunno."

"Then it's up to me?" Ben asked quietly.

" 'Fraid it is," Jess sighed. He was a fleshy man, low and heavy. "But there ain't no regulation against an ex-Sheriff riding with his friends, Anthony," he flashed. "Figger your play, and then let me know."

"Thanks, Jess. I'd like for you to ride down and look over the ground. I don't want any talk in later years about my jumping Caddo without cause."

"Reckon you got cause without Tommy," said Allman. "However, I'll ride with you."

He deciphered the writing in the sand, studied the unmistakable signs of a gun fight in the brush, and said he was convinced that Tommy Melvin had been murdered in cold blood by three men, one of whom had been Caddo Parker.

"I'll put that in legal form if you want," he shrugged. "It may come in handy."

"Do that."

Ben Anthony returned to Alice for fresh clothes, a shave, and a meal. Then he rode toward Harry Odell's. His plans were made. Caddo's outfit was too strong for him to jump out singlehanded, or with his handful of hired guards. He had to have help either from the ranchmen or from another town. If the cattlemen wouldn't back his play he would bring in his own fighters.

Harry listened with a sinking heart. Damn Caddo anyhow! Why hadn't the outlaw and Sledge heeded his warnings and let Anthony alone!

"Can I count on you?" Ben asked grimly.

Harry turned and poured both of them a drink before he answered. What a spot to be caught in?

"Do you think," he parried, "that you can get enough men to handle Caddo?"

"I'll get 'em—somewhere," Ben promised.

Harry bent over the bottle and glasses. Damn Ben Anthony, he would get them. Caddo had signed his own death warrant by attacking Ben's wagons and killing the drivers. Sledge would be drawn into the clean-up! Ben wouldn't stop until the whole job was finished.

"I got a special reason for coming to see you first," Ben said slowly. "There has been some talk going around. Some of it has foundation, partner. I think the best thing you can do is to get on your horse and ride with me to the other spreads."

Harry turned, his face paling. How much did Ben Anthony know? How much was he just assuming?

"You got off the main trail," Ben said quietly. "It's not too late to pull back. There's nothing wrong with this country that running out Sledge and Parker won't cure."

Harry Odell nodded. His brain was a tumult. He couldn't refuse this offer. But could he get by with changing sides? Could he just pick up his rifle and ride into town to fight Caddo Parker?

"I'll ride with you," he said. As yet he had no plan, but there must be some way. Time was the important thing. He must have a little time to figure.

They found Walt Earnest in the flats cursing at the absence of unbranded yearlings.

"We don't want you riding with us, Walt," Ben said. "We just want you to know what's going on."

"And why don't you want me riding with you?" demanded the white-mustached ranchman. He felt Ben Anthony did not have all the tact in the world. "I'm getting along in years, but I can still show you buttons how to shoot. I'm ready when you say the word."

The thin dark-faced Keith Maitland was next. He agreed readily.

"We've needed a leader," he said. "This has been brewing a long time." His suspicious eyes studied Odell. "We met at Walt's and agreed to an open range," he added curtly. "We haven't had it. Caddo isn't the only man we have to stop."

Harry Odell flushed. "Any insinuations, Keith?"

Keith's only reply was a shrug.

Ben Anthony put in. "Mebbe after we settle this Parker's hash, we can have a winter roundup, Keith," he said hurriedly. "I've got some boys who can work cattle. I'll lend 'em to you, and you can sweep the flats and divvy up the mavericks."

"It would be nice," mused Keith, "to lay my hand on a maverick." He refused to look at Odell.

Then he turned back to Ben. "Count us in," he said quietly. "Any time you say."

Harry and Ben rode on to the Camerons' in silence. Harry's heart was beating like a trip hammer. He hadn't realized how near he was to actual warfare with his neighbors. He had assumed, because they were withholding their suspicions, that he had been getting by with his share of the maverick running and the rustling. Now he knew better. Now he knew that he had only one chance, and that was to see that Caddo and Sledge were wiped out before they could incriminate him.

Alan Cameron listened grimly. "Are you ramrodding the spread?" he demanded of Ben.

"Harry and me are," Ben answered. He, too, was realizing how near his boyhood friend stood to disaster.

"I've lost stock myself, Alan," Harry put in, with all his usual convincing charm. "Because I haven't howled, the word has got around that I ain't hurt."

Alan nodded. Nothing in his face showed that he believed or disbelieved.

"Sure thing, Ben," he said lightly. "We ain't had enough excitement around here lately."

Ben and Harry rode on. The trail carried them by Fritz Warner's.

"We'll ask Fritz," Ben suggested.

Harry pulled back. "That damned German! He won't fight."

"We'll give him a chance," Ben shrugged.

Harry hesitated again. Then, with a chuckle at his own impudence, he dismounted and walked toward the corral, a half-step ahead of Ben. Fritz was toiling over a break in his corral fence. Melba came out on the front porch. Harry saw her, and waved, a grin parting his lips.

Fritz listened, then nodded, his broad face impassive. Melba watched from the porch. She had no idea, of course, what Ben and Harry wanted with her husband. But she had her fears.

Fritz, she knew, meant to kill Harry Odell. She dreaded even this meeting, with Ben there. Fritz Warner was a man who had been driven too far, and who meant to turn back.

But nothing happened; Ben and Harry rode away, and Fritz returned to his work. After a moment Melba carried a pitcher of milk to her husband.

They sat in the shade, and Fritz drank gratefully. "It is nice that you should think of me," he told her gently.

Melba flushed. "I'm up with the housework," she said. "Dinner is on. I thought I'd give you a jump with the fence."

"It is hard work," he mused, "and heavy."

"I'm no child," she scoffed. "I could swing an ax with Pappy any day."

He accepted her help. After a half-hour, her face red with perspiration, she asked him timidly what Anthony and Odell had come for.

"They are getting together," he answered calmly, "to go after Caddo Parker. They asked me to help."

"Are you going, Fritz?" Melba demanded, suddenly pale. He was not a fighting man. He was a slow, dogged worker. "Don't go," she begged. "You're not a man used to shooting a gun."

Fritz shrugged his broad shoulders. "Once before, I refused," he said in his slow monotone. "It was a mistake. I thanked them for their invitation. I will be honored to ride with my neighbors after such a man as Parker."

Melba's eyes flooded with tears as she bent over her work. She was proud of Fritz. He would ride with Ben Anthony and the Maitlands and the Camerons, and he would put up a good fight. Even if he didn't come back, she would be proud of him.

Harry was grateful for Ben Anthony's departure. Ben was an accusing shadow of the mistake he had made, of the evil partnership he had accepted. Alone in his house, he drank heavily, and weighed his chances of riding down this narrow middle ridge.

Perhaps Caddo Parker was the only one of the outlaw gang who knew Harry's affiliation. Perhaps Stubby Wright, but certainly no more. He had been that careful. Harry took his six-gun out of its holster and fondled it, longing for the nerve, and the skill, to shoot Caddo down before the night rider could speak.

That was the answer. These ranchmen and Ben would handle Caddo, Harry was sure of that. But they meant to take the outlaw and hang him. Before the noose went around his neck, Caddo would surely talk.

But how would Ben launch the attack? Would they take Caddo by surprise, perhaps asleep in his camp? Harry mulled over this. He had to see that a battle was fought, and that Caddo was killed in it. His fingers tightened on the gun butt. Perhaps he could even do that killing himself. Perhaps he could lead the man out and shoot him down before . . .

No, he couldn't do that! He poured himself another drink, and damned himself for being such a physical coward. That was as far beyond his powers as looking Caddo in the eye and shooting it out.

But the idea of a trap appealed to him. It would. If Caddo rode into an ambush, and a rifleman such as Ben Anthony got in the first shot . . .

Harry's eyes gleamed. That was it. They could set a trap for Caddo Parker. He downed another drink. He could set it himself. He needed to redeem his prestige among his neighbors. The way to silence their suspicions about his association with Caddo was to be the ringleader of an ambush that would spell Caddo's doom.

That should be easy. Caddo still trusted him. So did Sledge. Was there a chance of getting the banker in the same fell swoop! No, that was impossible. Sledge would never venture out on a night raid. But would Sledge be any more apt to reveal his association with Caddo Parker than Harry Odell himself? No. There was no need of worrying about Sledge. If Caddo was handled, shot down without indicting his two associates, Sledge would clutch his mortgage notes tightly, and keep his mouth as tight.

Harry's lips parted in a cunning smile. He did not have the nerve to outshoot Caddo, but he could outthink him.

He saddled his horse and rode over to Walt Earnest's. He had hoped to break this future father-in-law of his, and then offer a condescending assistance. That plan must be abandoned. And he must curry his future father-in-law's approval instead of waiting for the time when he could exact it by the force of rescuing dollars. Humbly he sought out the old ranchman for confirmation of his strategy and assurance of his aims.

"I know a man who rides with Parker," Harry explained. "He worked for you once—Pickett."

It was safe to use Pickett's name. Pickett was dead, killed by Caddo Parker. But few besides Harry Odell knew that.

Walt nodded. "He was a good rider. I hated to see him take up with Caddo's gang."

"He had to eat," justified Harry. "I've talked to Pickett some. He ain't got any stomach for Caddo's policies. I've halfway promised him a job. He said he'd quit Caddo in a minute to ride for me at thirty and keep."

"He would," Walt said quickly. "And would make you a good man."

"Pickett sits in well with Caddo. I got a notion about handling Caddo. I'll have my vaqueros bunch some stock, mine and yours, in the flats above the canyon. Pickett will pass the word along to Parker that here are prime pickings. Then Pickett will tip me off as to the night and time Caddo is coming through. We'll wait for 'em at the canyon mouth. We can shoot 'em down like popping ducks on the water."

Walt eyed Harry with mingled suspicion and admiration. "That sounds good to me. Can we depend on Pickett?"

"I'd bet my bottom dollar on him," shrugged Harry.

"Get Ben's say-so," Walt said firmly. "Ben's the man we got to look to in this valley."

Harry's face flushed. Never had he been as jealous of his friend as at that moment.

"But you got a smart notion," Walt conceded grudgingly. "It'll save us some bloodshed. And God knows we ain't got blood to spare."

With this faint praise Walt stalked off to his corral.

Harry grinned at Bess. "I don't rate so high, do I?"

"Nobody will ever take Ben's place with him," Bess said softly. "You'll have to get used to that, Harry."

"I can stand it," he shrugged.

She was lovely in a freshly ironed dress, and his eyes danced. "Let's walk to the well," he suggested.

Bess agreed. They walked to the grove of cottonwoods which

her mother had planted just after her marriage to Walt Earnest, and which now stood thirty feet high, eloquent testimony that time was gradually softening the severity of these rolling ridges.

There Harry caught her in his arms. "It's gonna be a long time till spring," he complained.

Bess Earnest did not fight him off. She couldn't do that. She had promised to marry Harry Odell, and she would see that promise through, even though she had learned in the mental torment of these past few days that it was not he but Ben Anthony who stirred her emotions to a boiling point. Other women in this country had made such mistaken engagements and made them work. There was never enough time in this country for a woman to be sure. Boys and girls grew up in such a rush. Before they knew their own minds, they were paired off in the long fight that a man and a woman had to face together—the dry seasons, the sudden blue northers, the overflowing creeks and draws when the rains came hurtling at long last, the market panics, the loneliness, and the unbending hauteur of the hills around them. Above all, the loneliness.

"Yes, it will be a long time," she agreed, a catch in her throat.

It would indeed. For, until spring, she would have the pain and confusion of knowing that she could turn back if she wished, and that Ben Anthony would answer the slightest wave of her hand. She would probably find the time harder to pass than would Harry. For Ben the hours would move slowest of all.

They returned to the house to find Walt Earnest back from the corral, oiling his rifle. Harry chatted a moment longer, and then rode on to town. He was pleased with his scheme, and with the quick approval by his future father-in-law. Some day Walt Earnest might learn to show him at least a casual respect.

In town, he sought Ben's reaction. The big man wasn't so sure. This wasn't his way of settling a fight.

"But," Harry argued. "We don't want blood shed and lives lost. Caddo will fight, you can be sure of that. This way we get the drop."

"I like to give a man a chance," Ben hedged.

"A wolf like Caddo Parker!" sneered Harry. "What chance did he give Tommy Melvin? Three to one, and that one a kid still wet behind the ears. Mebbe you don't value your own hide, Ben, but the rest of us do."

Ben agreed. When he learned that Walt Earnest had approved the scheme, he protested no further.

Now it was up to Harry to make sure Caddo would ride into the trap. He waited in the saloon until late afternoon, wondering if his plans would go awry because Caddo was off in Duval County. He didn't dare to question the loafers around Fatty's. Or Sledge.

He didn't want to face the banker's questioning stare. Caddo he could handle. Caddo still had the failing of trusting his fellow man.

Before dark Caddo swaggered in. He gave Harry a quick look, then ordered a drink. Harry edged up to him, speaking out of the side of his mouth.

"I've got two hundred head of Wide S stock bunched at the canyon mouth," he said slyly. "Ready to take 'em?"

"Any time," Caddo shrugged.

"Tomorrow night? About midnight?"

"What difference does the time make?"

"I'll have my riders posted," Harry explained oilily. "If trouble is coming, we can give you a warning."

"Suits me."

"Better bring your whole outfit."

"Why? Looking for trouble?"

"It's coming sooner or later," Harry shrugged. "That will just about clean up that flat land. No telling who you'll run into."

Caddo nodded. "I'll be there. Station your boys between the canyon and Walt Earnest's. If you hear any night riding, shoot three times."

Harry nodded. His dark eyes gleamed triumphantly as he mounted his horse and rode back to his ranch. Caddo was a trusting soul. Caddo was ready to ride into the end that always came to his kind.

Next day Harry and Ben Anthony made the rounds of the ranches, naming a place and time to meet, cautioning all to secrecy.

Jess Allman rode into the wagon yard as they were talking and Ben outlined their intentions to the Sheriff.

Harry Odell sketched a map on the ground. Caddo and his men must start the cattle through this canyon. Riflemen posted on the ridges should have an easy time.

"Count me in," Jess said.

"It's not your fight," Ben pointed out. "We're not paying you to be Sheriff."

"Some things," grinned Jess, "I can do for nothing. I need my job back. The sooner we get this country rid of Caddo Parker, the quicker you men can start paying your taxes."

"We can use you," said Ben unhesitantly. Jess Allman was turning gray about the temples, but he was still a good man in a fight.

"And Tuck Crawford," added Jess. Tuck had been his deputy through two terms of office. "Tuck wants to be around when there is any shooting."

Ben counted noses. That made nine.

"How many do you think Caddo will have?" he asked.

"Not over five or six. Caddo doesn't like to cut too many in."

"This is one time," Ben said grimly, "those who were left out won't kick."

12

THEY were ready to give Fritz Warner up when the stocky German came riding through the brush at a slow trot, his hunting rifle lying loosely over his knees in lieu of a scabbard. Harry Odell had made the sneering remark that Fritz was never around with a fight scheduled, and had proposed they go on. Ben insisted they wait until straight-up dark.

Keith Maitland broke the silence. "Howdy, Fritz."

Others murmured their greetings. Fritz Warner looked from face to face. "Sorry to be late," he apologized. "I had to ride into town for shells."

Maitland's lips curved in a smile. Out of shells! Other ranchmen kept them on hand by the boxful.

Their number had increased to twelve, for both Maitland and Cameron had brought relatives who were willing to risk their necks in this fight. Keith's two nephews were strapping replicas of himself, as tall and thin, as straight-lipped. Harry Odell chuckled to himself. The element of surprise in their favor, plus the weight of numbers. And probably of superior marksmanship. For Ben Anthony, he knew, could draw a fine bead, and there had never been a Maitland who was not a crack shot.

He hummed a little tune to himself. Maybe he was going to wriggle out of this hole after all. If so, he promised himself, it would be his last.

Reaching the gulch, they stopped for coffee and dried venison by the small spring where Harry had met Melba Melvin more than once. The cabin where they had held their last rendezvous, where Timothy had surprised him with a buffalo gun, was a stone's throw away. He recalled this, and his eyes mocked Fritz Warner's broad impassive face.

Harry sketched the canyon again, though there was not a man there who did not know every foot of this ground. They rode toward the mouth of the gulch in the late twilight and took up their stations.

"The higher we get up," said Ben Anthony, "the better chance we have of getting a shot. There'll be cattle in front of 'em. We'll have to shoot down at 'em."

"Give us our orders, Ben," said Keith Maitland.

"Sure," echoed Jess Allman. "This is your show."

Harry Odell's lips tightened. Already, in their admiration of Ben Anthony's physical powers, they had forgotten his part, which had been nothing more than planning the trap, and setting it.

"I could take that ledge up there," proposed Ben, waving upward. "I used to be fair at night shooting. And a downhill target doesn't bother me too much."

"We gotta have somebody at the back end," said Walt. "We don't want a damned one of 'em getting away."

The back mouth of the canyon was no more than fifty yards wide. Here was a level sandy surface, gradually yielding to the high shale walls. Every outfit in this valley had used the canyon at one time or another for a roundup of the flats. Nature seemed to have dropped it here in an odd moment of generosity, a corral fashioned out of sand and shale, and out of time.

"We'll let the cattle come on in, and the riders," said Ben. "Holding the mouth will be just a question of throwing the cattle back. They won't keep going into gunfire."

"We need our best shots up front," said Maitland, and waited confidently.

"Keith, suppose you and Rex fade me and Al up here," Ben suggested. "We'll start the shooting, boys. We'll wait until the drag men are in and try to cripple 'em with our first fire. Walt, you and Jess and my two boys hold back here. As soon as the drag men are through, run down and hold 'em in."

"Bueno," agreed Walt.

"The rest of you, hold down the trail," added Ben. "The cattle will turn off when you shoot in their faces. We'll keep 'em milling. The steers might hurt 'em more than our shooting."

No one noticed that something like a grin split Fritz Warner's face. So he was stationed with Harry Odell! He had hope for that. He was not a man who would challenge another in open gunfight. He had never practiced speed with a revolver and was only an average shot with a rifle. But he had learned that patience usually holds out its own reward.

Odell, Tuck Crawford, the two Cameron boys, and both of Keith Maitland's nephews rode after Fritz.

Ben climbed up the shale side, Alan Cameron at his heels. The canyon's floor still held a few slivers of pale daylight, and Ben approved of their layout. Once into the canyon, Caddo Parker and his men would have a devil of a time getting out. The walls would stop them on two sides. Blazing lead would close the entrance and the exit.

Ben and Al stretched out behind a mossy boulder. The light would be with them as soon as the moon came up. Now the mouth of the canyon was a long crooked black shadow.

"Hope Caddo don't come along before the moon does," murmured Al.

"He won't," Ben said confidently. "He and his boys are spoiled to moonlight."

The gloom of night was heavy upon the gulch where the vigilantes waited grimly for the first telltale clatter of moving cattle. The waiting was hard. No fires could be lit, no cigarette tips could be glowing. Each man sat quietly, but tensely, and passed the time examining his own thoughts.

Ben Anthony looked up at the shapeless streaked sky and guessed it was ten o'clock, and they would have two hours more to wait. Ben recalled the thrill of Bess Earnest's kiss, and thought of her approaching marriage to Harry Odell. Could he stand this country when Bess was another man's wife, and when Walt Earnest was dead and Harry was ramrodding the Wide S? Could he stand it even if he and Morgan Mann were making all the money Morgan expected? He doubted it. Much of the financial gain that had come to him had been thrust upon him, as if Fate were partially recompensing him for what had been taken away. A gambler who is indifferent to winning usually wins. Ben made swift calculations. If Morgan bought him out, he would have enough to buy a big spread farther west. He patted his rifle. Perhaps this was his last fight in the Chin-chin basin.

Farther out, waiting on horseback, Harry Odell twitched nervously, time after time examining the skies above him and wondering about the time. In an hour or so he would know his fate. Certainly the odds were in his favor. The four men stationed at the mouth of the canyon were crack rifle shots. Again, as always, he placed his faith in Ben Anthony. Ben would seek out Caddo Parker for his first shot, and if he had any kind of target, Caddo would never live to indict Harry Odell.

Harry grinned. He had certainly lived his life in the protecting shadow of this big man. How often had Ben fought his battles for him? Harry even looked back and regretted the remark he had made to Elizabeth Earnest about Ben's association with Melba Melvin—and it was unusual for him to regret anything except occasional failures to satisfy his own desires.

Sure that Caddo Parker would be out of the way very shortly, he thought about Marvin Sledge. There was a danger, of course. But it was doubtful if the ire of these aroused ranchmen would fall upon the banker's head. Sledge was suspected of buying stolen cattle from the outlaw for his tallow vats, but not of full complicity—not of engineering Caddo's raids, not of inspiring and financing the attacks on Ben Anthony's wagon. If Ben knew about the latter, Harry mused, Sledge's life wouldn't be worth a plugged nickel. Perhaps he and Sledge could make an agreement. In return for the banker's silence about Harry Odell's part in the skinning and tallow raids, Harry would keep mum about Sledge's guilt in the thefts and murders that had sent Ben on the warpath.

Sledge, like Odell, couldn't pull out. There was no use of it. Each had come out of these panic years with a profit. They would turn straight.

There were five in the group watching this narrowing back door to the canyon. A dark shape came close to Harry.

"Caddo ought to be along any minute," Harry said cheerfully.

"Yes," a calm voice answered almost in his ear.

Harry started. Fritz Warner! Why did Fritz have to be stationed so close to him? Harry patted his horse's flanks and moved away. He noticed that Fritz followed.

There was little room here. Harry moved again.

"Quit moving around," Tuck Crawford snapped. "You want to be heard?"

Harry obeyed. It was only nervousness anyhow, he assured himself. The German was too dumb to hold any malice, or to be dangerous if he did. Harry grinned to himself as he recalled Melba's frozen submission to him. He really had that gal's number. After a visit or two, she would warm up. Help pass the time until spring, when Bess Earnest would be his.

An hour had passed. High on the ledge Alan Cameron saw the moon peeping from between two deep banks of clouds.

"There it comes," he sighed in relief.

Ben Anthony nodded. Now the moonlight was playing hide-and-seek with the shadows around the canyon mouth. Soon the entire gulch would be flooded with orange brilliance. He recalled camping out here in his younger days, and seeing all the pale silvery glory of the night lanterns drop in heavy showers, caroming off the shale walls, and settling on the canyon's bottom in a deep shimmering pool.

"Listen!" Cameron breathed in his ear.

He listened a moment. Yes, cattle were moving in the flats a mile away. And a voice floated to them on the thin night air, a harsh voice snapping out orders.

"It won't be long," Cameron gloated.

"Don't get in a rush," Ben warned. "Hold our fire until the drag men are in. We want to settle this tonight."

Cameron murmured agreement.

Ben crouched over the boulder, listening intently, making out Caddo's progress from the sounds. The cattle would have drifted some. Riders were breaking through the brush on the ridges. Caddo, damn him, was a thorough workman. When he worked a ridge, he didn't leave a stray.

The moon crept higher. Ben saw a furtive shadow across the canyon, the shadow of a man. He hoped no warning would be given. Night riders like Caddo had sharp eyes, and an uncanny intuition. They could scent a trap sometimes in the dark.

It was hard to wait patiently. Ben knew that. His own nerves were on hair trigger's edge. But Caddo and his riders were still an hour away from the canyon mouth. Their drag men would come slower, holding the steers in close until the herd had struck its gait. Now they were milling the cows together, and the clatter came in a single sound, as if the herd was getting started. A shrill

"Ki, yi!" drifted up to them, and then the noise of a pistol shot, perhaps fired in the face of an angry steer trying to break away to the freedom of the brush.

Ben held his breath for fear this shot might touch off a fusillade from the cliffs. But evidently every man had recognized it for a pistol's explosion, and knew that it was not a signal to start shooting. They could see the two point riders come over the gentle swell of the gulch and into the moonlight bathing the entrance to the canyon. It was hard to hold back an itching trigger finger, but Ben let them come on. The drag men would be their first target.

Now the cattle. The sandy floor of the canyon quivered with the stomping of the aroused steers. They were well fed and watered; they were in a humor to fight back against this fan-shaped force of men prodding them ahead, swinging lariats in their faces, again discharging revolvers under their noses.

Ben Anthony sighted Caddo Parker. The outlaw leader was riding a point, and Ben had a dead bead on him as Caddo rode into a silver of moonlight. But Ben withheld his fire. That took all of his will power. For Tommy Melvin's sake, he would like to be the one who got Caddo.

There was a sudden scramble up the sides of the gulch by a handful of rebellious steers, and again Ben's force trembled. One of Caddo's riders plowed up within twenty yards of where Keith Maitland was hiding before turning the cattle back to the bottom.

"God dammit," moaned Cameron, his mouth against Ben's ear, "come on in there."

The dragmen, four of them, swung into the canyon. Now without open ground on either side, only ahead, the cattle moved more obediently. The point men pressed their sides in and—

"Now!" Ben Anthony told Al Cameron.

He had a bead on one of the drag men. His shot rang out over the noise of moving cattle and scraping horses and cursing men. His aim was true, and Al Cameron yelled hoarsely as his own target also dropped.

Both men shot again. And, across the canyon, Keith Maitland was as accurate.

The four drag men had ridden right into their line of fire, had been there exposed on all sides and flooded by deadly moonlight.

Three of them dropped quickly and a fourth lost his horse.

Ahead Walt Earnest and Jess Allman were also shooting. The outlaw riding ahead of the steers, swinging an oil lantern to guide the point men, simply melted from the saddle. No fewer than three rifles brought him down.

Caddo Parker, riding the left point, was spared this first annihilating burst of gunfire by the troublesome cattle themselves, and the screen of the far canyon wall.

"Break for cover, men!" he yelled. "There's hell to pay."

He set the example, spurring his horse up the bank of the gulch. He made a poor target as his horse whinnied in protest, and slipped on the rocky shale, floundering back five steps for every ten advanced.

Anthony saw him, and opened fire. But the range was too far. Closer, within pistol's distance, Walt Earnest cracked down, and Jess Allman turned his rifle on Caddo in support. The outlaw's horse screamed and leaped straight up. He threw himself out of the saddle in a desperate dive. His riddled horse turned over once in the air and then fell among the milling cattle, stone-dead.

Caddo tried going up the bank; but two shots whined close to him, and he gave up. He simply stiffened and went rolling back down the incline. Here, at the bottom of the canyon, under the shelter of the high bank, was protective darkness. Besides, there were milling, frightened steers plunging this way and that, infuriated by the noise and wild with excitement.

Caddo had lost his rifle. But he had his revolver, and he lay quiet against the bank hoping for a target. He saw a man dart down the bank, then another. He threw shots at both. Ben Anthony and Al Cameron had lead singing right by their ears, but neither was hit. A revolver makes a poor weapon for this kind of fighting. They reached the mouth of the canyon and now had the remnants of the gang hemmed in, including Caddo himself.

Caddo started shooting at the flashes. His gang had been reduced to four men, as many dropped in the first devastating fire from the ledge. He saw Stubby Wright dart among the milling cattle, screened by them from the fire above, and he tried to follow. Then, as Wright broke away from the steers, and toward the back entrance, Tuck Crawford and Ebbie Maitland charged him on horseback, firing right into his face. Wright went toppling, to be crushed under the weight of a frantic steer also trying to find a way out of this maelstrom of death and thunder.

Then Caddo knew he was hopelessly trapped. He and two of his riders were hemmed in this narrow canyon by superior forces who had both ends blocked, and both ledges manned. There was no accident about this trap. It had been a cold double-cross, carefully planned, expertly carried out. Caddo dived among the cattle as a shot rang close to him. Walter Earnest had had a glimpse of him from the canyon wall and was shooting like mad.

The riflemen on the cliffs were perfectly covered, but they had the disadvantage of shooting sharply downhill at blurred targets. It was hard to tell which was a steer and which was a man.

Caddo roared with rage.

"Harry Odell!" he yelled. "Where are you, Odell?"

He saw that his number was up. The hopelessness of his plight did not worry him. His kind knew such an end was coming, and preferred it to the business end of a swinging rope.

All Caddo thought about, and hoped for, was a chance to meet Odell face to face. One shot at Odell, and he was ready to cash in.

He rolled among the cattle, tossed and buffeted by their horns. He was thrown against one of his riders, a half-breed named Bostick, and heard the man scream as a sharp horn gored him. Bostick scrambled for the canyon, the steer hard after him. Caddo dived for the steer's horns, pulling the animal off, then wrestled precariously a moment himself until he could bring up his pistol. The steer dropped like a log from his shot.

But Bostick's relief was short-lived. The injured man tried to crawl up the ledge to safety, and, from fifty yards above, Jess Allman and Walt Earnest poured relentless lead into him. He slid back down, and this time it did not matter that an excited steer gouged him.

Caddo Parker was a target himself for a moment, but he reached the safety of the frightened herd, if that was a safety, with his pistol still in his hand. Again his voice bellowed out:

"Odell! Damn you, Odell, where are you!"

A longhorn pushed him over; a steer stepped squarely into his side and Caddo knew as he lurched to his feet that one or more ribs were broken. This was a pushing, surging mass of cattle. The lead steers had been turned back by the shooting at the yawning canyon's mouth, where Tuck Crawford and Harry Odell and Fritz Warner were stationed. Twice wild-eyed beasts almost broke through. Once Tuck Crawford turned an animal back at the risk of his own skin.

The crush was toward the middle, and in the middle, and Caddo Parker was hopelessly caught in its wave. Down he went, and he found at the bottom of the mass a relief from the pressure, as cattle were locked tight against one another, pushing, straining. He heard a yell behind him:

"Close in, men. Keep the cattle stirring."

No gang was ever wiped out more brutally. Ben Anthony and Al Cameron and Keith Maitland left their perches on the ledges and, shooting with pistols now, firing right into the faces of the bewildered beasts, kept them grinding, surging back and forth. Under their sharp frightened hoofs and desperate tossing horns died the last of Caddo's henchmen, died screaming in pain and fear, died appealing to his chief for aid.

There was Caddo alone, two hundred steers hemming him in. But Ben Anthony heard him shout again and again:

"Damn you, Odell! Come down here, Odell! I'll settle with you before I die."

Harry Odell heard, too. Harry followed Tuck Crawford and Ebbie Maitland as they obeyed Anthony's orders and closed in on the mass of cattle. Harry Odell heard, and his face went white.

Caddo knew he had broken bones. His body was racked in pain from his bare head to his boots. But he crawled among the steers toward the canyon mouth, still clutching his revolver. He had stopped shooting. There would be no chance in the squirming mass to reload, and, with the savage intentness of a doomed man, he was saving a shot for Harry Odell. Perhaps he would never reach the man who had betrayed him, but he would die trying.

Now the ranchmen had stopped shooting, except to turn the cattle back into the canyon, except to keep them grinding. Keith Maitland's face turned pale as he imagined the torturous death of Caddo's owl-hooters. He had never seen a punishment so grim, or so certain. Not one of them had even been wounded, and, indeed, few shots had been flung in their direction.

The steers were bunched in one distinct mass, scraping against

135

the shale sides, cutting the sandy bottoms to ribbons with their flailing hoofs. They bawled in fear and anger. There was no break in the bank of horns and rumps.

"Surely they're dead by now," sighed Maitland to Anthony. A cowman hated to deal out such a fate to fellow men, even to men like Caddo Parker. "Let's turn the steers loose."

In rebuttal to his argument, they heard Caddo's hoarse voice again, sounding as if it came from the other end of the canyon:

"Odell, damn you? Come to me, Odell. Lemme get my hands on you."

Ben Anthony shouted back in sudden fury. Always it had seemed to make him furious that he could not fight Harry Odell's battles.

"How about me, Parker? Keep yelling. I'll come to you."

And he started pushing through the first layers of tossing cattle.

"Come back, you danged fool!" yelled Maitland.

"Let the steers go," Ben shouted back. "I'll get Caddo."

Several beasts broke by him to freedom. Neither Maitland nor Cameron moved to stop them.

"Where are you, Parker?" shouted Anthony.

He had lost his gun. He was using both hands to push off the horns and whirling rumps.

"Over here, Anthony," Caddo roared. There was a shrillness in his voice. He was a hurt man. He could hardly keep on his feet even when cattle were not pressing against him. But he still had his gun, and his hate. And, as if guided by a higher fate, he was working his way painfully toward the open end of the canyon, to where Harry Odell sat trembling on his horse.

But not for long. Suddenly Harry whirled around and touched spurs to his horse. Caddo's hoarse voice was coming closer and closer. It was impossible that a man could come out of that awful certain death. But Caddo was coming, and shouting his threats.

A rider darted in swift quick pursuit. Neither Ebbie Maitland nor Tuck Crawford, pushing into the ranks of the steers themselves, heeded.

Fritz Warner had never ridden so hard before. But never before had he had such an incentive to ride.

13

A CHARGING longhorn bowled Caddo over. He yelled in fright, and clawed frantically. His revolver was knocked out of his hand, and he knew he could never retrieve it. Sharp hoofs tore at him, and it was a broken, bloody wreck of a man who pitched shakily to his feet, who rolled toward the canyon wall. He saw Ben across the sea of humps.

"Here, Anthony," he yelled. He had no strength left. He knew he would never walk again, if he could ever stand upright, but he had courage left, and a willingness to meet his fate. "I'm whipped, Anthony," he groaned. "But let me get to Odell. Let me lay my hands on Odell, and I'll give up."

The pressure of the steers was lessening as more and more of the insane beasts swept out of the canyon's mouth, and back into the brush. But this growing rush also brought a danger, a caroming steer had more momentum.

As Caddo crawled to his feet a longhorn caught him in the side, and down he went again. A scrawny muley turned upon him in wild fury, and he would have died then and there if the animal had possessed horns. As it was, he suffered additional torture from the raining hoofs, and could barely crawl away again, to the shale bank, where he leaned against the rocks and called out to Anthony in a weaker voice:

"Help me, Anthony," he begged. "Over here, Anthony. Over here for God's sake!"

Anthony heard him, and pushed through the bank of steers toward him. It was slow and painful progress. For every two steps he took, he was pushed back one.

At last he stumbled through a lane in the humps and horns and caught up the moaning Caddo.

"I'm all in, Anthony," moaned the outlaw. "Get me out of here. Take me anywhere. I'd rather hang than this, Anthony."

Ben held Caddo with one hand and started pushing along the canyon wall. Twice steers pressed him against the wall, and now he was a man with aches and gashes of his own. But he held grimly to his prisoner. Hanging to him, grateful for even this hand, Caddo kept croaking over and over again:

"Where's Odell? Why can't I see Odell?"

Now the milling steers had found a leader, a gaunt beast whose hide gleamed white in the moonlight. A giant of a beast, and wild with fury. It pushed its way through the cattle with sudden determination, and they gave before the sharpness of its horns and its power. Right toward Keith Maitland and Walt Earnest it charged, with other fright-mad steers behind it, and Walt did not escape in time. The gaunt longhorn caught him in the hip and tossed him high on the cliff. He came rolling back, but Keith Maitland, able to avert the rush, caught him and held on. Now the steers were sweeping ahead, and no hand could have stopped them.

Ben Anthony clung to the shale wall. Caddo was jerked from him once, but he recovered his prisoner with a desperate lunge.

Then Ben himself was slammed hard against the rocks, and Caddo slipped from his hands. Not until the last steer had stampeded out of the canyon did they find the outlaw.

And then he was beyond their punishment. Then he lay moaning, still alive, but with a bloody froth on his lips.

Keith Maitland reached him first and pulled up his head. But there was no recognition in Caddo's eyes. Not for a moment.

"Where's Odell?" he babbled. "Damn you, Odell, why can't I see you?"

Keith tried to pull him up. Caddo moaned in pain.

"He's cut and trampled to pieces," Keith told Jess Allman.

Now Ben was limping toward them. The big man was shaken up and bruised, but there were no deep gashes.

"Done for?" he asked quietly.

"On his way out," Keith confirmed. He added in a moment, with a genuine regret: "A helluva way for a man to die."

"Odell," babbled the dying man. "Odell."

138

Maitland bent over him again. "What's this about Odell?" he asked sharply.

"Odell," whimpered Caddo. "Double-cross. Lemme get . . . to Odell."

"Was Odell working with you?" demanded Keith.

Caddo did not answer. His eyes closed. Keith Maitland shook him roughly.

"Was Odell your man?" demanded the ranchman.

Caddo looked up. Some of the pain seemed to have left his face and eyes.

"You are sure rough . . . on a honest rustler," he murmured, a grin parting his lips.

He raised his head as if to speak further. Then he dropped back, and only Keith Maitland and Ben Anthony heard his last whisper.

"Odell, he's sure . . . a slick one."

Keith Maitland stood up. His eyes glared accusingly at Anthony.

"We got other work to do," he said grimly. "Where's this Odell?"

"What about Odell?" demanded Walt Earnest, limping up, putting much of his weight upon Jess Allman's shoulder.

"Caddo babbled about a double-cross," Keith growled. "I've had my hunches about Odell all along. He was working with Caddo."

Now Walt Earnest also looked to Ben Anthony. They knew the big man's loyalty toward his boyhood friend.

"Sure there was a double-cross," Ben said quickly. "Harry worked through a rider named Pickett who used to be Walt's man. They set this trap here, the two of them. Caddo rode into it. That's the double-cross Caddo meant."

"That's thin, Anthony," Keith snapped.

Now Alan Cameron came up, and Rex Maitland, and Tuck Crawford and Keith's nephews.

"Where's Odell?" demanded Keith. "We'll let him talk for himself."

"He was with us," volunteered Tuck. "Right by me most of the time."

"He ain't here now," Keith observed with a mirthless grin. "Looks like he'd want to stay around to count his chickens."

"Odell!" yelled Ben, giving a scornful look to Keith Maitland. There was no answer. "Harry!" he shouted again.

His booming voice rang out through the night. But still no reply. Keith Maitland's grin widened.

"We got another man missing," observed Jess Allman. "Who is it?"

A glance around told Anthony who was the other missing ranchman.

"Fritz!" he exclaimed.

"Might have known that damned German would turn yellow and run," growled Al Cameron.

"No," Ben said slowly. "He didn't run."

He took a step, then winced at the pain in his leg. "Let's break it up," he said gruffly. "Tomorrow's soon enough to bury the steers we lost. And Caddo's gang."

"What about Odell?" demanded Maitland. "I'm not taking your story, Anthony. I think Odell was in this up to his neck, and I'm not stirring a step until we reach some agreement."

Ben looked down at Keith Maitland with a deep unhappiness in his eyes.

"I reckon that can wait," he said gently.

"No!" snapped Cameron. "I'm with Maitland. I'll bet my bottom dollar it was Odell who drained these flats of unbranded stock."

"Mebbe," agreed Ben. He stood silent a moment, running his fingers through his unruly hair. He looked off. The loyalty of a lifetime dies hard. Harry Odell had been many things, as had most men. One man is seldom to another man what Odell had been to Anthony. But still a loyalty was only that, never a justification. Ben would never ask the question these men wanted to ask. Perhaps they were wrong. He didn't know for sure. Or did he? He could guess at much more than he did know.

"It can wait," he said curtly. "Fritz is entitled to the first crack at him."

It was a queer feeling. He was hoping that his guess was right, and that Fritz Warner had not fled from a fight with Caddo Parker's outfit because of his fear, but to take up a fight that was

140

his own, and that other men should not speculate upon. It was queer to stand there hoping that Fritz would accomplish his purpose, and that that finis would be Harry Odell's instead of the equally brutal end these men would deal out to him if they found him. He hoped Harry Odell wouldn't die cheap.

"What's Fritz got to do with it?" demanded Maitland.

"Don't ever ask him," shrugged Anthony. "Don't ever ask where he popped off to in the dark."

Fritz did not fire a shot. Even when the first wave of steers stumbled toward them, bawling furiously, groping in the dark of the night and their own fear for a way out of this canyon, he did not fire his rifle. Tuck Crawford did, and even Harry Odell, and Ebbie Maitland. They fired over the heads of the cattle and turned the longhorns back into a milling mass, and then waited grimly to see if any of Caddo's riders would get through the maelstrom.

None did, of course. Until Odell heard Caddo's hoarse voice, they never saw or heard a human being, only floundering rumps and menacing horns and dismayed bawling.

Fritz did not take his eyes off Odell. When Harry whirled his horse around and fled, the German was right after him.

He was no crack rider. Odell had a quick and easy start on him, and in a moment Fritz was pursuing only the clatter of hoofs ahead, with never more than a fleeting glimpse of Odell against the sky line. But Fritz kept the trail, and he kept his rifle ready. He did not have to be told that his chief virtue, and one of his precious few, was a slow, limitless patience.

Harry Odell rode like a wild man. For a time he rode in a crazy fear, babbles of curses breaking from his lips. Others must have heard Caddo's incriminating shouts, Caddo's hoarse accusations thrown from the very heart of the mass of cattle. Caddo's threats had thrown Harry into a panic. He gained on Fritz until he was far ahead.

He did not hear the first clattering pursuit. Perhaps Odell wouldn't have heard a dozen horses, he was so frightened. But, as he neared his own ranch, he slowed the pace of his chestnut horse, and began to look back upon what happened with some calmness. What did Caddo's shouts mean to Ben Anthony, the Maitlands,

Alan Cameron and Walt Earnest? Parker tried to reach him, shouting of a double-cross. But how incriminating was that? Could he bluff it out? Or should he hang out until morning, take what money he had deposited with Sledge, and leave?

He yearned for Ben Anthony's strength. The idea occurred to him that he might sell his ranch to Ben. But to sell out and run would mean the end of his plans to marry Bess Earnest and dominate the Chin-chin basin!

He reached his gate, by now a full mile ahead of Fritz Warner, who was not the rider and did not have the horse to stay within hailing distance. The thing to do, he had decided, was to go to San Antonio and draw upon Sledge for money. Or Anthony would send it to him. More than ever he would have to depend upon Anthony—to stake him—to find out whether it was safe for him to return to Alice.

He had poured himself a drink when Fritz Warner clattered up to his gate.

"Who's there?" Harry shouted.

"Warner," the German answered. "Come out, Odell."

So completely had Harry Odell underestimated this stolid man that he did not hesitate. He stepped out the front door, holding his drink in his hand.

"What do you want, Fritz?" he demanded sharply. His only feeling was resentment that Fritz was presuming to break in upon his privacy. At the moment he had no inkling of fear. He would have laughed had he been told that Fritz Warner had followed him here to kill him.

Fritz stepped closer. Harry had lit a single lamp, and the light here on the porch was pale and flickering. But it was strong enough for him to see what was in the German's face.

"Fritz, what's the matter with you?" he asked sharply. He backed toward the door. "Fritz, are you crazy?"

There was no answer. Fritz took a step forward.

"Let me get my gun," Harry quavered. "I'll step right in here and—"

"Do you need a gun, Odell?" Fritz Warner asked quietly.

"What do you mean?" Harry exclaimed.

"This," Fritz growled. And he leaped.

Harry Odell tried to thrust off the clutching hands. But Fritz

142

was a strong man, almost as broad as he was tall. His muscles were hard from long hours of backbreaking labor. Harry was like a match in his hands.

The German saw this, and laughed.

"You are afraid, no?" he taunted.

Harry's breath came in heavy gasps. "Lemme get my gun," he panted. "Gimme a fighting chance, Warner. My gun—it's—Oh!"

His exclamation, his plea, died off in a stifled scream. For Fritz Warner's strong fingers had found his throat, and Harry Odell was being pushed backward against the porch floor.

Melba heard the horse, and then her husband's slow footsteps. She heard him fumbling in the kitchen, and the scraping of his match. She turned with a sigh.

She had slept fitfully. All sorts of wild dreams had disturbed her. First she had seen Fritz lying wounded, bleeding to death, while Harry Odell bent over him and laughed cruelly. Then she had seen Fritz falling over the canyon cliffs, tumbling over and over. And she was leaping after him, clutching at his whirling body, begging him to come back.

Thank God, he was safe! He had come back.

"Melba, Melba!"

His was a funny pronunciation. He made two words out of her name, calling, "Mel-ba, Mel-ba."

"Yes, Fritz," she answered sleepily.

"You should get up, Melba. You should get up and make us some coffee."

"It isn't that late," she whined. "It's still dark."

"Who cares what time it is?" her husband demanded. "We sleep late tomorrow, Melba. I do not go to work on the range."

She rolled out of bed and pulled her kimono around her. Fritz was standing in the doorway holding up the lamp. She blinked at him. He held a bottle of wine in his hand.

"See this, Melba?" he chortled. "It is old wine. It came from the old country. It is wine such as the noblemen drink. My father brewed it. I helped tread the grapes which made it when I was only a child. Would you like a glass of wine, Melba?"

She came into the kitchen, still asleep. Fritz caught her in a rough hug, and his whiskers scraped against her cheek.

"Fritz, what on earth!" she demanded. "You're acting like a crazy man."

He held aloft the bottle. "We drink to us, Melba. We drink to our life."

"What happened! Why are you so happy of a sudden?"

His face sobered.

"I feel," he said slowly, "that tonight is our wedding night."

14

BEN ANTHONY did not share in the "cleaning up." He did not help bury Caddo Parker, nor Caddo's gang. Early the next morning, his heart heavy, his shoulders stooped as if he were carrying a heavy load, he left with two wagons for Duval County, winding among the trails to Encinal and Cotulla before returning.

Deliveries were quick, new orders were easier. Ben left his two drivers to return alone and pushed his bay aimlessly down the San Antonio road. He stopped for the night at San Diego, the sleepy Duval town that numbered only a half-dozen Americans among its inhabitants. His agent told him that a lieutenant from Fort Sam Houston in San Antonio had been there searching for him the day before, and had left word for Ben to come to San Antonio immediately.

Ben journeyed up through Tilden and the Nueces bottoms, stopping over at George West to transact a large-scale deal with West himself, whose operations were bigger than those of all the Chin-chin outfits combined. Reaching San Antonio on the third day, he asked for Lieutenant Westcott and was presently shaking hands with a slim young man who had West Point written all over him.

Westcott, he learned, was the new supply officer for the area. A week ago Ben's heart would have leaped almost out of his flannel shirt. This surely meant the freighting contact from Brownsville and Port Isabel that he had sought so eagerly. But now it was hard to get excited over material things.

"You're a hard man to locate, Mr. Anthony," smiled the officer. "You gave me quite a chase, and then I never could catch up with you."

Ben nodded. He *had* been traveling fast. He had been trying to ride away from something, a something that always kept pace with him.

"We have your bid on our freighting from Isabel and Brownsville to San Antonio," continued Lieutenant Westcott. "It is low. We have two transports arriving in Isabel next week bearing artillery emplacements. We are replacing all of our present guns at Sam Houston, at Fort Concho, and at Forts Stanton and Sumner in New Mexico. That represents a pretty big freighting order. Can you handle it?"

Ben nodded. "Yes, sir."

"Can you give me a price?"

"Not at once. There are numerous factors to be considered."

"Of course," agreed the lieutenant. "We will furnish you with infantry escort from San Antonio to New Mexico."

"I can make you a price on per-mile basis," Ben proposed.

"That is good enough."

"My regular price, eight cents a mile per hundred."

The officer made a quick mental estimate. "Railroads are cheaper, Mr. Anthony," he frowned.

"But they don't run in that direction," Ben grinned. "I'm making only a fair margin of profit, Lieutenant Westcott, you can be sure of that. You can be sure, too, I'm hauling government freight just as cheaply as I would for a private individual. I'm not trying to get fat on Uncle Sam."

"You're one of the few men we deal with who aren't," growled Westcott. "I'll take your terms on the artillery emplacements as well as the supplies. Now I have another proposal. Don't you haul hay to strategic points along a trail herd's route?"

"I haul anything anywhere," Ben said quickly.

"We need ten thousand beef cattle," Westcott continued. "I don't know where we'll get them yet. I was thinking of contacting either the West or the King ranches."

Ben shifted his weight. "I'm not trying to horn in on anybody else's business," he said, "but I can contract for the cattle, too."

"Oh, are you a ranchman? I didn't realize you were so versatile, Mr. Anthony."

"No. But around Alice, where I make my headquarters, there are a half-dozen outfits dying for such a contract. All of the cattle sold in that country for the last two years has been going for hides and tallow. My ideas is to take your contract and split it among them. Give 'em all a bit of the government's cash. They need it."

"We Army men," sighed Westcott, "aren't used to dealing with ethics. We last paid thirty-five dollars per animal, Mr. Anthony."

Ben's eyes gleamed. This meant three hundred and fifty thousand dollars for the stricken ranchmen of the Chin-chin basin.

"I'd like to have that—for my neighbors," he said. "I'll guarantee delivery. And you'll get the pick of their herds, not the culls."

"Which we mostly have—in the past," Westcott smiled.

"You'll get two-year-olds, the best on the Jim Wells range," Ben promised. "I'll throw the hay in, lieutenant, if you'll let me have that cattle contract."

"You're a generous man, Mr. Anthony," laughed Lieutenant Westcott. "It's a pleasure to do business with you. We'll sign that contract."

"Aw, I ain't giving anything away, lieutenant," Ben grinned. "My future is in this country. My capital is invested in it. When my neighbors do well, I do well."

"Such a philosophy," the officer dryly answered, "would be the salvation of the world."

Ben reached Alice shortly after dark and turned in at his wagon yard. Agatha Melvin saw him, and left her dish washing to put a tender steak on the stove. When he came into the restaurant, she had it sizzling-hot.

It was the first time he had seen her since he had found Tommy's body among the mesquites, riddled with bullets from outlaw guns.

"Ben Anthony, where have you been?" she demanded. "Everybody in this country has been worrying themselves sick about you."

"Had a trip to make," he said crisply. His reasons for leaving so abruptly, and staying away so long, were his own. He had never been able to figure out things except on the trail. When a man was rolled in his blankets and smoking his last cigarette while his campfire burned low, the answers to things that bothered him came easier. Life was simple and straight—out there.

"Walt Earnest has been in nearly every day. And Keith Maitland. They're waiting on you to hold a meeting."

"What for?"

"You poor boy!" sighed Mrs. Melvin. "You don't know about Harry Odell, do you?"

"No," admitted Ben.

There was an empty feeling inside him as he waited for her explanation. He knew, and yet he didn't.

"He was found dead. Killed on his own front porch." Mrs. Melvin's eyes closed in horror. "Strangled to death," she added.

Ben's lips tightened. Strangled. Naturally Fritz wouldn't know how to use a gun. No one had ever considered him dangerous, because he lacked a six-gun hanging at his side. Sometimes this country plumb forgot there were other weapons.

"What's that to do with me?" he demanded. His voice was purposefully gruff. To delay learning about this, he had spent six days and nights on the trail.

"Well, who's to take over Odell's ranch?" Mrs. Melvin countered. "There are no heirs. Not a soul to leave it to. And it's some of the best grazing land in this country."

"As good as any," Ben nodded.

Mrs. Melvin leaned forward, straining to conceal her excitement.

"Who's to run it, Ben?"

"I don't know," Ben shrugged.

"Why not you?"

"Me?"

"Who has a better claim?" she said triumphantly. "Harry owed you money, didn't he?"

"Only a little," Ben said slowly.

"Even Keith Maitland," Mrs. Melvin went on, "agrees you should have it."

"It's hardly up to them," Ben snapped. "Doesn't a man get buried before they start splitting up his land?"

He finished his dinner in silence, brooding upon this suggestion that he take over his dead friend's spread. After eating he walked across to the saloon for a drink. Jess Allman hailed him from the courthouse, and immediately brought up the question of the Dollar Mark.

"There are some taxes against it," he explained. "Two years. It's customary, when there are no heirs, to let the land revert to the state. In which case there will be a public sale. That will be bad for this country, Anthony, in more ways than one. Suppose an outsider came in. As Sheriff, I'm administrator of the estate. If you'll file your claim, I'll have to hold a county sale. In which case nobody will bid against you."

"That sounds like a frame-up," Ben said.

"It is," Allman snapped. "You lost dough because of Caddo Parker and Sledge."

"What about Sledge? What has happened?"

"That's another reason we were plumb anxious for you to get back," the Sheriff said. "Sledge holds notes against these ranches. Right now he's in San Antonio."

Ben looked questioningly at him.

"Yes," Allman chuckled, "he left kinda sudden. By agreement, so to speak. Nobody had anything on Sledge, but he agreed real quick he had better move—for his health. This low country don't agree with him."

"I won't miss him," Ben murmured.

"He brought up the question of these notes," continued the heavy-set Sheriff. "They gotta be paid. The boys in the valley are hoping you'll buy up those notes from Sledge, Ben."

"I doubt if I have the cash."

"Sledge," murmured Allman, a quirk to his lips, "agreed to discount 'em some. In fact, Ben, Sledge turned out to be a plumb generous man. I think you can take up the paper all right."

"I see," Ben chuckled.

"Now let's belly up," suggested the Sheriff, "and you tell me what *you* know."

They turned to the bar. Before Ben had emptied his glass Keith Maitland rode up with one of his nephews, Ebbie. Keith's quick friendly greeting surprised Ben. He had considered their alliance as one of necessity.

Keith turned to Ebbie. "Ride out to Walt Earnest's and tell Walt, Ben is in town," he ordered. "We'll settle this tonight."

"I want to see Walt, too," grinned Ben. "I got a present for you boys. You wanna sell some cattle?"

"For hides and tallow!" scoffed Maitland. "I'll starve first, Anthony."

"No, to the Army," Ben said. "They're buying again. I got an order in my pocket here." And he explained.

Keith Maitland's face brightened a moment, then he shook his head. "That's good for you, Ben," he said curtly. "The Dollar Mark is overstocked. I think some of the yearlings belong to us, but that doesn't matter. We can't prove it."

"I didn't get this contract for myself," Ben declared. "My idea is to split it between you, Walt Earnest, and Al Cameron."

"How big is the order?"

"Ten thousand head."

"How much?"

"Thirty-five per." Ben waited a moment, then added: "I promised the Army we'd send 'em prime stuff for that."

"Boy howdy!" Keith agreed. "We'll tie red ribbons around their necks for that."

He studied Ben's face. "You ain't wolfing, Ben?"

"No. Walt has the biggest outfit. Say Walt sells four thousand, you and Al three each."

"Most of the young stuff," Keith said bitterly, "has a Dollar Mark brand on it."

"We can figger out something about that," Ben suggested.

They turned to the bar for another drink. It was a full hour before Walt Earnest came limping into the saloon. His leg still troubled him.

"Damn you, Ben," he exploded, "why don't you tell a body where you're going!"

"Sometimes, Walt, I don't want 'em to know."

He told Earnest about his army order, and how he proposed to fill it. Walt Earnest's white mustaches bobbed. As did his white head.

"That'll see us through," he said huskily. "That will put this country on its feet again."

"And me, too," Ben said cheerfully. "I'll buy up Sledge's notes. And all of you owe me and Morgan. We'll start cashing in ourselves."

"What about Odell's spread?" demanded Keith.

"Mebbe that can be split between you," Ben shrugged. "I don't want it."

"Don't want it!" exclaimed Maitland. "Don't want a ranch!"

"Not that way," Ben said firmly.

"I don't reckon Ben needs it," Walt drawled. "I got other plans for him."

"I got other plans for myself," Ben said crisply. "I told you a few years back I was doing my own thinking, Walt."

"So you were," Walt chuckled. "I said you *were*."

Ben stared at the old man. Usually such arguments brought out Walt's flaming temper. But Walt was in a bubbling good humor.

"I can't bring you around to my way of thinking, Ben Anthony," continued Walt Earnest. "I've been trying to get you to give up this danged freight line and this store and come back where you belong—to the Wide S. You know better than me, of course. You're brash and full of vinegar, and no old-timer can tell you what's good for you."

"That's right," Ben said quickly. Why did they have to have such arguments every time they met!

"But there's somebody over at the hotel who can set you straight," Walt chuckled. "Go over there and tell *her* you're running your own affairs and to stay the hell out of them. Go on!"

"Bess!" guessed Ben, his voice a weak gasp.

"You're blamed tooting!" Walt said triumphantly. "Go on over there if you ain't scared. She rode in with me, and she's got her talk all mapped out."

Ben's face crimsoned before Walt's cackle and Keith Maitland's thin smile and Jess Allman's twinkling eyes.

"To hell with you guys!" he blurted. "I'll bet you cooked this up just to get a chance to hurrah me."

Walt Earnest gripped his shoulder, then turned on Maitland. "I'll buy this round," the Wide S owner offered. "I got the jump on you boys from here on. I got a riding boss who can handle cattle."

"You got a good one," agreed Maitland. "Here's to him!"

Ben turned and stumbled out of the saloon. So she was waiting in the hotel! He clomped back up the street as fast as his high-heeled boots would permit.

She was in the sitting room idly turning the pages of a San Antonio newspaper. She looked up at his entrance, and there was written in her face what he wanted to know. There was only one question, in fact, that he couldn't see the answer to right there within the four walls of this room.

Who wanted to buy some slightly used freight wagons and some stout stagecoaches!

Curtis Bishop was born in Tennessee but lived most of his life in Texas, where he traveled with rodeos and worked for several daily newspapers as a feature writer. Much of his newspaper writing dealt with characters, landmarks, and institutions of the Old West. In 1943 he also began writing fiction for the magazine market, especially Fiction House magazines, including *Action Stories*, *North-West Romances*, and *Lariat Story Magazine*. During World War Two, Bishop served with the Latin-American and Pacific staffs of the Foreign Broadcast Intelligence Service. His first attempt at a novel was titled "Quit Texas—or Die!" in *Lariat Story Magazine* (3/46). Subsequently he expanded this story to a book-length novel titled *Sunset Rim*, published by Macmillan in 1946. "Bucko-Sixes—Wyoming Bound!", which appeared in *Lariat Story Magazine* (7/46), was expanded to form *By Way Of Wyoming*, also published in 1946 by Macmillan. These were followed by *Shadow Range* (Macmillan, 1947), an expansion of "Hides for the Hang-Tree Breed" in *Lariat Story Magazine* (11/46). Although Bishop continued to write for the magazine market for the rest of the decade, his next novel didn't appear until 1950 when E. P. Dutton published *High, Wide And Handsome* under the pseudonym Curt Brandon. The pseudonym was necessary because Macmillan claimed it owned all rights to the Curtis Bishop name for book publication. *Bugles Wake* by Curt Brandon followed, published by E. P. Dutton in 1952. *Rio Grande* under the byline Curtis Bishop was published in 1961 by Avalon Books, the last of his Western novels. Living in Austin, Texas for much of his life, where he was able to study many of the documents of early Texas on deposit at the University of Texas' Special Collections, Bishop's Western fiction is informed by a faithfulness to factual history and authentic backgrounds for his characters, while he also was able to invest his stories with action and a good deal of dramatic excitement.